"Our engagement?" Jodi checked him angrily. **"What engagement? We aren't engaged...."**

"Not officially...but..."

"Not in any way," Jodi interrupted Leo fiercely.

"Jodi, I had no choice," Leo told her quietly. "You were seen leaving my suite early in the morning. Apparently..."

"I know what you're going to say." Jodi stopped him. "I was seen leaving your hotel room, so I must be some kind of fallen woman. Totally unfit to teach school. For heaven's sake, all I've done is go to bed with you—*twice....*"

DO NOT
Disturb

Anything can happen behind closed doors!

Do you dare find out…?

Welcome again to DO NOT DISTURB!

Meet Leo as he finds a gorgeous siren
in his hotel room…. In fact, Leo's bedmate
is Jodi Marsh, a schoolteacher—
who's just got the wrong room!
But when the mix-up leads to passion,
they definitely *don't* want to be disturbed!

Read on, as bestselling Presents® author
Penny Jordan pens a tantalizing tale
of unexpected passion…
and heart-stopping romance!

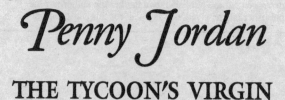

Penny Jordan

THE TYCOON'S VIRGIN

DO NOT Disturb

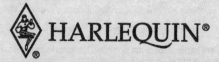

HARLEQUIN®

TORONTO • NEW YORK • LONDON
AMSTERDAM • PARIS • SYDNEY • HAMBURG
STOCKHOLM • ATHENS • TOKYO • MILAN • MADRID
PRAGUE • WARSAW • BUDAPEST • AUCKLAND

ISBN 0-373-12260-8

THE TYCOON'S VIRGIN

First North American Publication 2002.

Copyright © 2002 by Penny Jordan.

CHAPTER ONE

'MMM.' Jodi could not resist sneaking a second appreciative look at the man crossing the hotel lobby.

Tall, well over six feet, somewhere in his mid-thirties, dark-suited and even darker-haired, he had an unmistakable air about him of male sexuality. Jodi had been aware of it the minute she saw him walking towards the hotel exit. His effect on her was strong enough to make her pulse race and her body react to him in a most unusual and un-Jodi-like manner, and just for a second she allowed her thoughts to wander dreamily in a dangerous and sensual direction.

He turned his head and for a shocking breath of time it was almost as though he was looking straight at her; as though some kind of highly intense, personal communication was taking place!

What was happening to her?

Jodi's heart, and with it her whole world, rocked precariously on its oh-so-sturdy axis; an axis constructed of things such as common sense and practicality and doing things by the book, which had suddenly flung her into an alien world. A world where traitorous words such as 'love at first sight' had taken on a meaning.

Love at first sight? Her? Never. Stalwartly, Jodi dragged her world and her emotions back to where they belonged.

It must be the stress she was under that was causing her to somehow emotionally hallucinate!

'Haven't you got enough to worry about?' Jodi scolded herself, far more firmly than she would ever have scolded one of her small pupils. Not that she was given to scolding them very much. No, Jodi loved her job as the headmistress and senior teacher of the area's small junior school with a passion that some of her friends felt ought more properly to be given to her own love life—or rather the lack of it.

And it was because of the school and her small pupils that she was here this evening, waiting anxiously in the foyer of the area's most luxurious hotel for the arrival of her cousin and co-conspirator.

'Jodi.'

She gave a small sigh of relief as she finally saw her cousin Nigel hurrying towards her. Nigel worked several miles away in the local county-council offices and it had been through him that she had first learned of the threat to her precious school.

When he had told her that the largest employer in the area, a factory producing electronic components, had been taken over by one of its competitors and could be closed down her initial reaction had been one of disbelief.

The village where Jodi taught had worked desperately hard to attract new business, and to prevent itself from becoming yet another small, dying community. When the factory had opened some years earlier it had brought not just new wealth to the area, but also an influx of younger people. It was the children of these people who now filled Jodi's classrooms. Without them, the small village school would have to close. Jodi felt passionately about the benefits her kind of school could give young children. But the local authority had to take a wider view; if the school's pupils fell below a certain number then the school would be closed.

Having already had to work hard to persuade parents to support the school, Jodi was simply not prepared to sit back whilst some arrogant, uncaring asset-stripper of a manufacturing megalomaniac closed the factory in the name of profit and ripped the heart out of their community!

Which was why she was here with Nigel.

'What have you found out?' she asked her cousin anxiously, shaking her head as he asked her if she wanted anything to drink. Jodi was not a drinker; in fact she was, as her friends were very fond of telling her, a little bit old-fashioned for someone who had gone through several years at university and teacher-training college. She had even worked abroad, before deciding that the place she really wanted to be was the quiet rural heart of her own country.

'Well, I know that he's booked into the hotel. The best suite, no less, although apparently he isn't in it at the moment.'

When Jodi exhaled in relief Nigel gave her a wry look. 'You were the one who wanted to see him,' he reminded her. 'If you've changed your mind...?'

'No,' Jodi denied. 'I have to do something. It's all over the village that he intends to close down the factory. I've already had parents coming to see me to say that they're probably going to have to move away, and asking me to recommend good local schools for them when they do. I'm already only just over the acceptable pupil number as it is, Nigel. If I were to lose even five per cent of my pupils...' She gave a small groan. 'And the worst of it is that if we can only hang on for a couple more years I've got a new influx due that will take us well into a good safety margin, providing, that is, the factory is still operational. That's why I've got to see this...this...'

'Leo Jefferson,' Nigel supplied for her. 'I've managed to talk the receptionist into letting me have a key to his suite.' He grinned when he saw Jodi's expression. 'It's OK, I know her, and I've explained that you've got an appointment with him but that you've arrived early. So I reckon the best thing is for you to get up there and lie in wait to pounce on him when he gets back.'

'I shall be doing no such thing,' Jodi told him indignantly. 'What I want to do is make sure he understands just how much damage he will be doing to this village if he goes ahead and closes the factory. And try to persuade him to change his mind.'

Nigel watched her ruefully as she spoke. Her high-minded ideals were all very well, but totally out of step with the mindset of a man with Leo Jefferson's reputation. Nigel was tempted to suggest to Jodi that a warm smile and a generous helping of feminine flirtation might do more good than the kind of discussion she was obviously bent on having, but he knew just how that kind of suggestion would be received by her. It would be totally against her principles.

Which was rather a shame in Nigel's opinion, because Jodi certainly had the assets to bemuse and beguile any red-blooded man. She was stunningly attractive, with the kind of lushly curved body that made men ache just to look at her, even if she did tend to cover its sexy female shape with dull, practical clothes.

Her hair was thick and glossily curly, her eyes a deep, deliciously dark-fringed, vibrant blue above her delicately high cheekbones. If she hadn't been his cousin and if they hadn't known one another since they had been in their prams he would have found her very fanciable himself. Except that Nigel liked his girlfriends to treat flirtation and sex as an enjoyable game. And Jodi was far too serious for that.

At twenty-seven, she hadn't, so far as Nigel knew, ever had a serious relationship, preferring to dedicate herself to her work. Nigel knew that there were more than a handful of men who considered that dedication to be a total waste.

As she took the key card her cousin was handing her Jodi hoped that she was doing the right thing.

Her throat suddenly felt nervously dry, and when she admitted as much to Nigel he told her that he'd arrange to have something sent up to the suite for her to drink.

'Can't have you driven so mad by thirst that you raid the mini-bar, can we?' he teased her, chuckling at his own joke.

'That's not funny,' Jodi immediately reproved him.

She still felt guilty about the underhanded means by which she was gaining access to Leo Jefferson's presence, but according to Nigel this was the only way to get the opportunity to speak personally with him.

She had originally hoped to be able to make an appointment, but Nigel had quickly disabused her of this idea, telling her wryly that a corporate mogul such as

Leo Jefferson would never deign to meet a humble village schoolteacher.

And that was why this unpleasant subterfuge was necessary.

Ten minutes later, as she let herself into his hotel suite, Jodi hoped that it wouldn't be too long before Leo Jefferson returned. She had been up at six that morning, working on a project for her older pupils, who would be moving on to 'big' school at the end of their current year.

It was almost seven o'clock, past Jodi's normal evening-meal time, and she felt both tired and hungry. She stiffened nervously as she heard the suite door opening, but it was only a waiter bringing her the drink Nigel had promised her. She eyed the large jug of brightly coloured fruit juice he had put down on the coffee-table in front of her a little ruefully as the door closed behind the departing waiter. Good old plain water would have been fine. Her mouth felt dry with nervous tension and she poured herself a glass, drinking it quickly. It had an unfamiliar but not unpleasant taste, which for some odd reason seemed to make her feel that she wanted some more. Her hand wobbled slightly as she poured herself a second glass.

She read the newspaper she had found on the coffee-table, and rehearsed her speech several times. Where was Leo Jefferson? Tiredly she started to yawn, gasping with shock as she stood up and swayed dizzily.

Heavens, but she felt so light-headed! Suspiciously she focused on the jug of fruit juice. That unfamiliar taste couldn't possibly have been alcohol, could it? Nigel knew that she wasn't a drinker.

Muzzily she looked round the suite for the bathroom. Leo Jefferson was bound to arrive soon, and she wanted to be looking neat and tidy and strictly businesslike when he did. First impressions, especially in a situation like this, were very important!

The bathroom was obviously off the bedroom. Which she could see through the half-open door that connected it to the suite's sitting room.

A little unsteadily she made her way towards it. What on earth had been in that drink?

In the suite's huge all-white bathroom, Jodi washed her hands, dabbing cold water on her pulse points as she gazed uncertainly at her flushed face in the mirror above the basin before turning to leave.

In the bedroom she stopped to stare longingly at the huge, comfortable-looking bed. She just felt so tired. How much longer was this wretched man going to be?

Another yawn started to overwhelm her. Her eyelids felt heavy. She just had to lie down. Just for a little while. Just until she felt less light-headed.

But first…

With the careful concentration of the inebriated, Jodi removed her clothes with meticulous movements and folded them neatly before sliding into the heavenly bliss of the waiting bed.

As Leo Jefferson unlocked the door to his hotel suite he looked grimly at his watch. It was half-past ten in the evening and he had just returned to the hotel, having been to inspect one of the two factories he had just ac-

quired. Prior to that, earlier in the day, he had spent most
of the afternoon locked in a furious argument with the
now ex-owner of his latest acquisition, or rather the ex-
owner's unbelievably idiotic son-in-law, who had done
everything he could at first to bully and then bribe Leo
into releasing them from their contract.

'Look, my father-in-law made a mistake. We all make
them,' he had told Leo with fake affability. 'We've
changed our minds and we no longer want to sell the
business.'

'It's a bit late for that,' Leo had replied crisply. 'The
deal has already gone through; the contract's been
signed.'

But Jeremy Driscoll continued to try to browbeat Leo
into changing his mind.

'I'm sure we can find some way to persuade you,' he
told Leo, giving him a knowing leer as he added, 'One
of those new lap-dancing clubs has opened up in town,
and I've heard they cater really well for the needs of
lonely businessmen. How about we pay it a visit? My
treat, we can talk later, when we're both feeling more
relaxed.'

'No way,' was Leo's grim rejection.

The gossip he had heard on the business grapevine
about Jeremy Driscoll had suggested that he was a seedy
character—apparently it wasn't unknown for him to try
to get his own way by underhanded means. At first Leo
had been prepared to give him the benefit of the doubt—
until he met him and recognised that Jeremy Driscoll's
detractors had erred on the side of generosity.

A more thoroughly unpleasant person Leo had yet to
meet, and his obvious air of false bonhomie offended

Leo almost as much as his totally unwarranted and unwanted offer of bought sex.

The kind of place, any kind of place, where human beings had to sell themselves for other people's pleasure had no appeal for Leo, and he made little attempt to conceal his contempt for the other man's suggestion.

Jeremy Driscoll, though, it seemed, had a skin of impenetrable thickness. Refusing to take a hint, he continued jovially, 'No? You prefer to have your fun in private on a one-to-one basis, perhaps? Well, I'm sure that something can be arranged—'

Leo's cold, 'Forget it,' brought an ugly look of dislike to Jeremy's too pale blue eyes.

'There's a lot of antagonism around here about the fact that you're planning to close down one or other of the factories. A man with your reputation...'

'Oh, I think my reputation can stand the heat,' Leo replied grittily.

He could see that his confidence had increased Jeremy's dislike of him, just as he had seen the envy in the other man's eyes when he had driven up in his top-of-the-range Mercedes.

Out of the corner of his eye he caught sight of the newspaper that Jeremy had rudely continued to read after Leo's arrival. There was an article on the page that was open detailing the downfall of a politician who had tried unsuccessfully to sue those who had exposed certain tawdry aspects of his private life, including his visits to a massage parlour. The fact that the politician had claimed that he had been set up had not convinced the jury who had found against him.

'I wouldn't be so sure about your reputation if I were

you,' Jeremy warned Leo nastily, glancing towards the paper as he spoke.

Giving him a dismissive look, Leo left.

Leo frowned as he walked into his suite. There was no way in a thousand years he was going to change his plans. He had worked too hard and for too long, building up his business from nothing…less than nothing, slowly, painstakingly clawing his way up from his own one-man band, first overtaking and then taking over his competition as he grew more and more successful.

The Driscoll family company was in direct competition to Leo's. Since their business duplicated his own, it was only natural that he should have to close down some of their four factories. As yet Leo had not decided which out of the four. But as for Jeremy Driscoll's attempt to get him to back out of the deal…!

Tired, Leo strode into the suite without bothering to switch on the lights. At this time on a June evening there was still enough light in the sky for him not to need to do so, even without the additional glow of the almost full moon.

The bedroom wasn't quite as well-lit; someone—the maid, he imagined—had closed the curtains, but the bathroom light was on and the door open. Frowning over such sloppiness, he headed towards the bathroom, closing the door behind him once he was inside.

Giving his own reflection a brief glance in the mirror, he paused to rub a lean hand over his stubble-darkened jaw before reaching for his razor.

Jeremy Driscoll's bombastic arrogance had irritated him to an extent that warned him that those amongst his family and friends who cautioned that he was driving himself too hard might have something of a point.

Narrowing the silver-grey eyes that were an inheritance from his father's side, and for whose piercingly analytical and defence-stripping qualities they were rightly feared by anyone who sought to deceive him, he grimaced slightly. He badly needed a haircut; his dark hair curled over the collar of his shirt. Taking time out for anything in his life that wasn't work right now simply wasn't an option.

His parents professed not to understand just where he got his single-minded determination to succeed from. They had been happy with their small newsagent's business.

His parents were retired now, and living in his mother's family's native Italy. He had bought them a villa outside Florence as a ruby-wedding present.

Leo had visited them, very briefly, early in May for his mother's birthday.

He put down his razor, remembering the look he had seen them exchange when his mother had asked wistfully if there was yet 'anyone special' in his life.

He had told her with dry humour that not only did his negative response to her maternal question relate to his present, but that it could also be applied indefinitely to his future.

With unusual asperity she had returned that if that was the case then it was perhaps time she paid a visit to the village's local wise woman and herbalist, who, according to rumour, had an absolutely foolproof recipe for a love potion!

Leo had laughed outright at that. After all, it was not

that he couldn't have a partner, a lover, if he so wished. Any number of stunningly attractive young women had made it plain to him both discreetly and rather more obviously that they would like to share his life and his bed, and, of course, his bank account... But Leo could still remember how at the upmarket public school he had won a scholarship to the female pupils had been scornfully dismissive of the boy whose school uniform was so obviously bought secondhand and whose only source of money came from helping out in his parents' small business.

That experience had taught Leo a lesson he was determined never to forget. Yes, there had been women in his life, but no doubt rather idiotically by some people's standards, he had discovered that he possessed an unexpected aversion to the idea of casual sex. Which meant...

Unwantedly Leo remembered his body's sharply explicit reaction to the woman he had seen in the hotel foyer as he had crossed it on his way to his meeting earlier.

Small and curvy, or so he had suspected, beneath the abominable clothes she had been wearing.

Leo's mother did not have Italian blood for nothing, and, like all her countrywomen, she possessed a strong sense of personal style, which made it impossible for Leo not to recognise when a woman was dressing to maximum effect. This woman had most certainly not been doing that at all. She had not even really been his type. If he was prepared to admit to a preference it was for cool, elegant blondes. Most definitely not for delectably sexy, tousled and touchable types of women, who turned his loins to hotly savage lust and even distracted his mind to the extent that he had almost found himself deviating from his set course and thinking about walking towards her.

Leo never deviated from any course he set himself—ever—especially not on account of a woman.

With an indrawn breath of self-disgust, Leo stripped off his clothes and stepped into the shower.

As a teenager he had played sports for his school, which, ironically, had done wonders to increase his 'pulling power' with his female schoolmates, and he still had the powerful muscle structure of a natural athlete. Impatiently he lathered his body and then rinsed off the foam before reaching for a towel.

Once dry, he opened the bathroom door and headed for the bed. It was darker now, but still light enough, thanks to the moonlight glinting through the curtains, for him not to need to switch on the light.

Flipping back the bedclothes, Leo got into the bed, reaching automatically for the duvet, and then froze as he realised that the bed—*his* bed—was already occupied.

Switching on the bedside lamp, he stared in angry disbelief at the tousled head of curly hair on the pillow next to his own—a decidedly female head, he recognised, just like the slender naked arm and softly rounded shoulder he could now see in the lamplight.

The nostrils of the proudly aquiline nose he had inherited from his mother's Italian forebears flared fastidiously as they picked up the smell of alcohol on the softly exhaled breath of the oblivious sleeping form.

Another scent—a mixture of warm fresh air, lavender

and a certain shockingly earthy sensuality that was Jodi's alone—his senses reacted to in a very different way.

It was the girl from the foyer. Leo would have recognised her anywhere, or, rather, his body would.

Automatically his brain passed him another piece of information. Jeremy Driscoll's oily-voiced suggestiveness as he had tried to persuade Leo to go back on their contract. Was this…this girl the inducement he'd had in mind? She had to be. Leo could not think of any other reason for her presence here in his bed!

Well, if Jeremy Driscoll dared to think that he, Leo, was the kind of man who…

Angrily he reached out to grasp Jodi's bare arm in strong fingers as he leaned across her to shake her into wakefulness.

Jodi was fathoms-deep asleep, sleeping the sleep of the pure of heart—and the alcohol-assisted—and she was having the most delicious dream in which she was, by some means her sleeping state wasn't inclined to question, wrapped in the embrace of the most gorgeous, sexy man. He was tall, dark-haired and silver-eyed, with features reassuringly familiar to Jodi, but his body, his touch, were wonderfully and excitingly new.

They were lying together, body to body, on a huge bed in a room with a panoramic view of a private tropical beach, and as he leaned towards her and stroked strong fingers along her forearm he whispered to her, 'What the hell are you doing in my bed?'

Her brain still under the influence of her 'fruit cocktail' Jodi opened bemused, adoring eyes.

Why was her wonderful lover looking so angry? Smiling sleepily up at him, she was about to ask him, but somehow her attention became focused on how downright desirable he actually was.

That wonderful naked golden-brown body. Naked. Yummy! More than yummy! Jodi closed her eyes on a sigh of female appreciation and then quickly opened them again, anxious not to miss anything. She watched the way the muscles in his neck corded as he leaned over her, and the sinewy strength of his solid forearms, so very male that she just had to reach out and run an explorative fingertip down the one nearest to her, marvelling at the difference between it and her own so much softer female flesh.

Leo couldn't believe his eyes—or his body. She, the uninvited interloper in his bed, was brazenly ignoring his angry question and was actually daring to touch him. No, not just touch, he acknowledged as his body reacted to her with a teeth-clenching jerk that gave an immediate lie to his previous mental use of the word 'unwanted'. What she was doing—dammit—was outright stroking him, caressing him!

Torn between a cerebral desire to reject what was happening and a visceral surge of agonisingly intense desire to embrace it, and with it the woman who was tormenting him with such devastating effectiveness, Leo made a valiant struggle to cling to the tenets of discipline and self-control that were the twin bastions of his life. To his shock, he lost. And not just the campaign but the whole war!

Jodi, though, fuelled now by something far more subtle than alcohol, and far stronger, was totally oblivious to everything but the delicious dream she had found her way into.

Imagine. When she touched him, like so, the most extraordinary tremors ran right through his whole body—and not just his, she acknowledged as she considered the awesome fact that her own body was so highly responsive, so reactive to every movement of his.

She was so lucky to be here with him on this wonderful private island of love and pleasure. Tenderly she leaned forward and flicked her tongue-tip delicately against the hollow at the base of his throat, revelling in the sensation of his damp skin against her tongue, its texture, its taste, the way that fierce male pulse thudded to life at her touch.

Leo couldn't believe what was happening. What she was doing; what he was letting her do. He found himself lying back against the pillow as she was the one to arch provocatively over him, whilst her tongue busily and far too erotically laved his skin.

Even in the less than half-light of the shadowy bedroom he could see the naked outline of her body with its narrow waist and softly flaring hips; her legs were delectably shaped, her ankles tiny and delicate, the shadowy triangle of hair between her thighs so soft and tempting that...

His throat dry with angry tension and gut-wrenching longing, Leo felt his whole body shudder.

He could see her breasts, soft, rounded, creamy-skinned, with darkly tender crests and tormentingly erect nipples.

Unable to stop himself, he lifted his hands carefully, cupping them. He could feel their warm weight, and he could feel, too, the tight hardness of those wanton peaks, tauntingly challenging him to...

Jodi gasped and then shivered in delight as she felt the rough pressure of her lover's tongue against her nipple.

'Oh, it feels so good,' she whispered to him, closing her eyes as she gave herself up to the sensations he was arousing. Her hand slipped distractedly from his arm to her own body, flattening betrayingly against her belly as she drew in a juddering breath of delirious pleasure.

Leo could scarcely believe the sheer wantonness of her reaction to his touch. He tried to remind himself that she was there for a purpose, doing the job she had been hired for, but his senses were too drugged to allow him to think rationally.

He had known then, in that fleeting second he had seen her in the hotel foyer, that she could affect him like this; that he would want her like this, no matter what the stern voice of his conscience was trying to tell him.

His hand slid to the curve of her waist and flared possessively over her hip, which fitted as perfectly into his grip as though they had been made for each other.

Her hands were on his body, their touch somehow innocently explorative, as though he was the first man she had ever been so intimate with—which was a ludicrous thought!

The soft whispers of female praise she was giving him had to be deliberately calculated to have the maximum effect on a man's ego—any man's ego—he tried to remind himself. But somehow he couldn't stop touching her—couldn't stop *wanting* her!

Jodi sighed blissfully in a sensual heaven. He seemed to know instinctively just how and where to caress her, how to arouse and please her. Her body soared and melted with each wonderful wave of erotic pleasure. Voluptuously she snuggled closer to him shivering in heady excitement as she let her hands wander at will over his body—so excitingly different from her own.

The bedclothes, which she had pushed away an aeon ago so that she could look at the powerful nakedness of the male body she was now so hungry for, lay in a tangled heap at the bottom of the bed. Moonlight silvered her own body, whilst it turned the larger and more muscular shape of her lover's into a dark-hued steel.

She ached so much for him. Her hands moved downwards over him, her gaze drawn to his taut, powerful magnificence.

Deliberately she drew her fingertips along the hard length of his erection, closing her eyes and shuddering as a deep thrill twisted through her.

Leo couldn't understand how he was letting this happen! It went totally against everything he believed in! Never before in his life had he experienced such intense and overwhelmingly mindless desire, nor been so driven by the fierce pulse of it to take what he was being so openly offered.

Every single one of his senses was responding to her with an uncheckable urgency that left his brain floundering.

The scent, the sight, the feel of her, her touch against his body, even the soft, increasingly incoherent sound of her husky, pleading moans, seemed to strike at a vulnerability inside him that he had never dreamed existed.

He reached out for her, giving in to the need burning through him to kiss every delicious woman-scented inch of her, and then to do so all over again, slowly and thoroughly, until the unsteadiness of her breathing was a torment to his senses. He finally allowed himself the pleasure of sliding his fingers through the soft, warm tangle of curls concealing her sex, stroking the flesh that lay beneath and slowly parting the outer covering of her to caress her with full intimacy.

She felt soft, hot, moist and so unbelievably delicate that, ignoring the agonised urging of her voice against his ear, he forced himself to love her slowly and carefully.

He could feel her body rising up to reach his touch as she writhed frantically against him, telling him in broken words of open pleasure that jolted like electricity through his senses just what she wanted from him and how. She somehow managed to manoeuvre both of them so that he was pushing urgently against her and then inside her, as though the intimacy was beyond his own physical control.

She felt. She felt…

Jodi heard the low, visceral male sound he made as he entered her, filled her, and sharp spirals of intense pleasure flooded her body.

Just hearing that sound, knowing his need, was almost as erotically exciting as feeling him move inside her. Long, slow, powerful thrusts lifted and carried her and caused her to reach out for him, drawing him deep inside her. The pleasure of feeling her body expand to accommodate him was so indescribably precious that she cried out aloud her joy in it and in him. She loved this feeling of being wrapped around him, embracing him, holding him, somehow nurturing and protecting his essential male essence.

Somewhere on the periphery of his awareness, Leo recognised that there was something that his mind should be aware of, something important his body was trying to tell him, something about both the intensity of what he was experiencing and the special, close-fitting intimacy of the tender female body wrapped around his own. But the age-old urgency of the need now driving him was short-circuiting his ability to question anything.

All he knew was how good she felt, how right, how essential it was that he reciprocate the wonderful gift she was giving him by taking them both to that special place that lay so tantalisingly almost within reach…another second, another stroke, another heartbeat.

He felt her orgasm gripping her; spasm after spasm of such vibrant intensity that its sheer strength brought him to his own completion.

As she lay in his arms, her body trembling in the aftershock of her pleasure, her damp curls a wild tangle of soft silk against his chest, he heard her gasping shakily, 'That was wonderful, my wonderful, wonderful lover.'

And then as he looked down into her eyes she closed them and fell asleep, with all the speed and innocence of a child.

Broodingly Leo studied her. There was no doubt in his mind that she was a plant, bought and paid for with Jeremy Driscoll's money.

And he, idiotic fool that he was, had fallen straight into the trap that had been set for him. And he suspected, now that he had time to think things through properly, that this was something more than Jeremy Driscoll supplying him with a bedmate for the night.

Jeremy was simply not that altruistic. Not altruistic in any way, shape or form, and Leo knew that he had not mistaken the dislike and envy in the other man's eyes earlier in the day. Jeremy knew that he, Leo, was not about to change his mind. Not unless Jeremy Driscoll believed he had some means of forcing him to do so.

Now, when it was too late, Leo remembered the newspaper article Jeremy Driscoll had been reading,

For a man in his position, an unmarried man, the effect of a public exposé, a woman selling her kiss-and-tell story to one of the national newspapers, would not be devastating. But Leo would be pilloried as a laughing stock for being so gullible and, as a result, would lose respect in the business world. If that happened he would not be able to count on the support and belief he was used to. No businessman, not even one as successful as Leo, wanted that.

He got out of bed, giving Jodi a bitter look as he did so. How could she lie there sleeping so peacefully? As though…as though… Unable to stop himself, Leo felt his glance slide to her mouth, still curved in a warmly satisfied smile. Even in her sleep she was somehow managing to maintain the fiction that what had happened between them was something special. But then no doubt she was a skilled actress. She would have to be.

The reality of what he had done pushed relentlessly through his thoughts. His behaviour had been so totally alien that even now he couldn't imagine what had possessed him. Or, at least, he could, but he couldn't understand how he had allowed it to get so out of control.

Or why he was standing beside the bed and continuing to look at her, when surely his strongest urge ought to be to go and have a shower as hot and strong as he could stand until he had washed the feel, the scent, the taste of her off his body and out of his senses. But for some incomprehensible reason that was the last thing he wanted to do…

Just in time he managed to stop himself from reaching out to touch her, to stroke a gentle fingertip along that tender cheekbone and touch those unbelievably long, dark lashes, that small, straight nose, those soft, full lips.

As though somehow she sensed what he was thinking, her lips parted on a sweetly sensual sigh, her mouth curling back into another smile of remembered pleasure.

What the hell was he doing, letting her sleep there like that? By rights he ought to wake her up and throw her out. He glanced at the alarm clock supplied by the hotel. It was two o'clock in the morning, and he told himself that it was because of his inbred sense of responsibility that he could not bring himself to do so.

It just wasn't safe for a woman—any woman, even a woman like her—to wander about on her own so late at night; anything could happen to her!

But he wasn't going to get back in that bed with her. No way!

Going into the bathroom, he pulled on the complimentary robe provided by the hotel and then made his way into the sitting room, closing the bedroom door behind him as he did so and snapping on the light.

The first thing he saw was the almost empty cocktail jug and the glass Jodi had drunk from.

Grimacing, he pushed it to one side. She had even had the audacity to order a drink on Room Service. Because she had needed the courage it would give her to go to bed with him?

He warned himself against falling into the trap of feeling sorry for her, making excuses for her. She had known exactly what she was doing... Exactly... He frowned as he moved a little uncomfortably in his chair.

He was wide awake now and he had some work he could be doing. When his would-be seducer woke up they were going to need to have a short, sharp talk.

There was no way he was going to allow Jeremy Driscoll to blackmail him into backing out of the contract he had made with his father-in-law.

Still frowning, he reached for his briefcase.

CHAPTER TWO

RUBBING her eyes, Jodi grimaced in disgust at the sour taste in her mouth. Her head ached, and her body did too, but they were different sorts of aches; the ache in her body had a subtle but quite distinctly pleasurable undertone to it, whilst the one in her head...

Cautiously she moved it and then wished she had not as a fierce, throbbing pain banged through her temples.

Instinctively she reached across, expecting to find her own familiar bedside table, and then realised that she was not in her own bed.

So where exactly was she? Like wisps of mist, certain vague memories, sounds, images, drifted dangerously across her mind. But no, surely she couldn't have? Hadn't! Frantically she looked to the other side of the large bed, the sledgehammer thuds of her heart easing as she saw to her relief that it was empty.

It had been a dream, that was all, a shocking and unacceptable dream. And she couldn't imagine how or why... But... She froze as she saw the quite unmistakable imprint of another head on the pillow next to her own.

Shivering, she leaned closer to it, stiffening as she caught the alien but somehow all-too-familiar scent of soap and man rising from the pillow.

What had been vague memories were becoming sharper and clearer with every anxious beat of her heart.

28

It was true! Here in this room. In this bed! She had. Where was he? She looked nervously towards the bathroom door, her attention momentarily distracted by the sight of her own clothes neatly folded on a chair.

Without pausing for logical thought she scrambled out of the bed and hurried towards them, dressing with urgency whilst she kept her gaze fixed on the closed bathroom door.

She longed to be able to shower and clean her teeth, brush her hair, but she simply did not dare to do so. Appallingly explicit memories were now forcing themselves past the splitting pain of her alcohol-induced headache. She couldn't comprehend how on earth she could have behaved in such a way.

She had been drinking, she reminded herself with disgusted self-contempt. She had been drinking, and whatever had been in that potent cocktail Room Service had sent up to the suite had somehow turned her from the prim and proper virginal woman she was into a...an amorous, sexually aggressive female, who...

Virginal! Jodi's body froze. Well, she certainly wasn't that any more! Not that it mattered except for the fact that, driven by her desire, she hadn't taken any steps to protect her health or to prevent...

Jodi begged fate not to punish her foolishness, praying that there would be no consequences to what she had done other than her own shocked humiliation.

Picking up her handbag, she tiptoed quietly towards the bedroom door.

Leo was just wondering how long his unwanted guest intended to continue to sleep in *his* bed, and whether or not five a.m. was too early to ring for a room-service breakfast, when Jodi reached for the bedroom door.

Even though his body ached for sleep, he had been furiously determined not to get back into his bed whilst she was in it. One experience of just how vulnerable he was to her particularly effective method of seduction was more than enough.

Even now, having had the best part of three hours of solitude to analyse what had happened, he was still no closer to understanding why he had been unable to stop himself from responding to her, unable to control his desire.

Yes, he had felt that bittersweet pang of attraction when he had first seen her in the hotel foyer, but knowing what she was ought surely to have destroyed that completely.

He tensed as he saw the bedroom door opening.

At first, intent on making her escape, Jodi didn't see him standing motionlessly in front of the window.

It was light now, the clear, fresh light of an early summer morning, and when she did realise that he was there her face flushed as sweetly pink as the sun-warmed feathers of clouds in the sky beyond the window.

Leo heard her involuntary gasp and saw the quick, despairing glance she gave the main door, her only exit from the suite. Anticipating her actions, he moved towards the door, reaching it before her and standing in front of it, blocking her escape.

As she saw him properly Jodi felt the embarrassed heat possessing her body deepen to a burning, soul-scorching intensity. It was him, the man she had seen in the foyer, the man she had thought so very attractive, the man who had made her have the most extraordinarily uncharacteristic thoughts!

Out of the corner of her eye Jodi could see the coffee-table and the telltale cocktail jug.

'Yes,' Leo agreed urbanely. 'Not only have you illegally entered my suite, but you also had the gall to run up a room-service bill. Do you intend to pay personally for the use of my bed and the bar, or would you prefer me to send the bills to Jeremy Driscoll?'

Jodi, who had been staring in mute distress at the cocktail jug, turned her head automatically to look at him as she heard the familiar name of her least favourite fellow villager.

'Jeremy?' she questioned uncertainly.

Jeremy Driscoll's father-in-law might own the local factory, and Jeremy himself might run it, but that did not make him well-liked in the locale. He had a reputation for underhand behaviour, and for attempting to bring in certain cost-cutting and potentially dangerous practices, which thankfully had been blocked by the workers' union and the health and safety authority.

But what he had to do with her present humiliating situation Jodi had no idea at all.

'Yes. Jeremy,' Leo confirmed, unkindly imitating the anxious tremor in her voice. 'I know exactly what's going on,' he continued acidly. 'And why you're here. But if you think for one minute that I'm going to allow myself to be blackmailed into giving in…'

Jodi swallowed uncomfortably against the tight ball of self-recrimination and shame that was lodged in her throat.

Did Leo Jefferson—it had to be him—really think that

she was the kind of person who would behave in such a way? His use of the word 'blackmail' had particularly shocked her. But was the truth any easier for her to bear, never mind admit to someone else? Was it really any more palatable to have to say that she had been so drunk—albeit by accident—that she simply had not known what she was doing?

To have gone to bed with a complete stranger, to have done the things she had done with him, and, even worse, wanted the things she had wanted with him... A woman in her position, responsible for the shaping and guiding of young minds...

Jodi shuddered to think of how some of the parents of her pupils, not to mention the school's board of governors, might view her behaviour.

'Well, you can go back to your paymaster,' Leo Jefferson was telling her with cold venom, 'and you can tell him, whilst you might have given me good value for his money, it makes not one jot of difference to my plans. I still have no intention of cancelling the contract and allowing him to buy back the business.

'I have no idea what he hoped to achieve by paying you to have sex with me,' Leo continued grimly and untruthfully. 'But all he gave me was a night of passably good if somewhat over-professionalised sex. If he thinks he can use that against me in some way...' Leo shrugged to underline his indifference whilst discreetly watching Jodi to see how she was reacting to his fabricated insouciance.

She had gone very pale, and there was a look in her eyes that under other circumstances Leo might almost have described as haunted.

Jodi fought to control her spiralling confusion and to make sense out of what Leo Jefferson was saying. She was going to avoid thinking about his cruelly insulting personal comments right now. They were the kind of thing she could only allow herself to examine in private. But his references to Jeremy Driscoll and her own supposed connection with him were totally baffling.

She opened her mouth to say as much, but before she could do so Leo was exclaiming tersely, 'I don't know who you are or why you can't find a less self-destructive way of earning a living.'

Ignoring the latter part of his comment, Jodi pounced with shaky relief on his 'I don't know who you are'.

If he didn't know who she was, she certainly wasn't going to enlighten him. With any luck she might, please fate, be able to salvage her pride and her public reputation with a damage-limitation exercise that meant no one other than the two of them need ever know what had happened.

She had abandoned any thought of pursuing her real purpose in seeking him out. How on earth could she plead with him for her school's future now? Another burden of sickening guilt joined the one already oppressing her. She had not just let herself down, and her standards, she had let the school and her pupils down as well. And she still couldn't fully understand how it had all happened. Yes, she had had too much to drink, but surely that alone...

Cringing, she reflected on her reaction to Leo Jefferson when she had seen him walking across the hotel foyer the previous evening. Then, of course, she had not known who he was. Only that…only that she found him attractive…

She felt numbed by the sheer unacceptability of what she had done, shamed and filled with the bleakest sense of disbelief and despair.

Her lack of any response and her continued silence were just a ploy she was using as a form of gamesmanship, Leo decided as he watched her, and as for that anguished shock he had seen earlier in her eyes, well, as he had good cause to know, she was an extremely accomplished performer!

'I have to go. Please let me past.'

The soft huskiness of her voice reminded Leo of the way she had moaned her desire to him during the night. What the hell was the matter with him? He couldn't possibly still want her!

Even though he had made no move to stand away from the door, Jodi walked towards it as determinedly as she could. She had, she reminded herself, faced a whole roomful of disruptive teenage pupils of both sexes during her teacher training without betraying her inner fear. Surely she could outface one mere man? Only somehow the use of the word 'mere' in connection with this particular man brought a mirthless bubble of painful laughter to her throat.

This man could never be a 'mere' anything. This man…

She had guts, Leo acknowledged as she stared calmly past him, but then no doubt her chosen profession would mean that she was no stranger to the art of making a judicial exit.

It went against everything he believed in to forcibly constrain her, even though he was loath to let her go without reinforcing just what he thought of her and the man who was paying her.

Another second and she would have been so close to him that they would almost have been body to body, Jodi recognised on a mute shudder of distress as Leo finally allowed her access to the door. Expelling a shaky, pent-up breath of relief, she reached for the handle.

Leo waited until she had turned it before reminding her grimly, 'Driscoll might think this was a clever move, but you can tell him from me that it wasn't. Oh, and just a word of warning for you personally: any attempt to publicise what happened between us last night and I can promise you that any ridicule I suffer you will suffer ten times more.'

Jodi didn't speak. She couldn't. This was the most painful, the most shameful experience she had ever had or ever wanted to have.

But it seemed that Leo Jefferson still hadn't finished with her, because as she stepped out into the hotel corridor he took hold of the door, placing his hand over hers in a grip that was like a volt of savage male electricity burning through her body.

'Of course, if you'd been really clever you could have sold your story where it would have gained you the highest price already.'

Jodi couldn't help herself; even though it was the last thing she wanted to do, she heard herself demanding gruffly, 'What…what do you mean?'

The cynically satisfied smile he gave her made her shudder.

'What I mean is that I'm surprised you haven't tried to bargain a higher price for your silence from me than the price Driscoll paid you for your services.'

Jodi couldn't believe what she was hearing.

'I don't...I didn't...' She began to defend herself instinctively, before shaking her head and telling him fiercely, 'There isn't any amount of money that could compensate me for what...what I experienced last night.' And then, before he could say or do anything more to hurt her, she managed to wrench her hand from his and run down the corridor towards the waiting lift.

A girl wearing the uniform of a member of the hotel staff paused to look at her as Jodi left Leo's suite, but Jodi was too engrossed in her thoughts to notice her.

Leo watched her go in furious disbelief. Just how much of a fool did she take him for, throwing out a bad Victorian line like that? And as for what she had implied, well, his body had certain very telltale marks on it that told a very different story indeed!

To Jodi's relief, no one gave her a second glance as she hurried through the hotel foyer, heading for the exit. No doubt they were used to guests coming and going all the time.

'Stop thinking about it,' she advised herself as she stepped out into the bright morning sunlight, blinking a little in its brilliance.

The first thing she was going to do when she got home, Jodi decided as she drove out onto the main road, was have a shower, and the second was to compose the letter she would send to Leo Jefferson, putting to him the case for allowing the factory to remain open—there was no way she was going to try to make any kind of personal contact with him now!

And the third: the third was to go to bed and catch up on her sleep, and very firmly put what had happened between them out of her mind, consign it to a locked and deeply buried part of her memory that could never be accessed again by anyone!

Jodi opened the front door to her small cottage, one of a row of eight, built in the eighteenth century, with tiny, picturesque front gardens overlooking the village street and much longer lawns at the rear. After carefully locking up behind her she made her way upstairs.

It was the sound of her telephone ringing that finally woke her; groggily she reached for the receiver, appalled to see from her watch that it was gone ten o'clock. Normally at this time on a Saturday morning she would be in their local town, doing her weekly supermarket shop before meeting up with friends for lunch.

As luck would have it, she had made no such arrangement for today, as most of her friends were away on holiday with their families.

As her fingers curled round the telephone receiver her stomach muscles tensed, despite the fact that she knew it was impossible that her caller could be Leo Jefferson; after all, he didn't even know who she was, thank goodness! A small *frisson* of nervous excitement tingled through her body, quickly followed by a strong surge of something she would not allow herself to acknowledge as disappointment when she recognised her cousin Nigel's voice.

It was no wonder, after all she had been through, that

her emotions should be so traumatised that they had difficulty in relaying appropriate reactions to her.

'At last,' she could hear Nigel saying cheerfully to her. 'This is the third time I've rung. How did it go with Leo Jefferson? I'm dying to know.'

Jodi took a deep breath; she could feel her heart starting to pound as shame and guilt filled her. The hand holding the receiver felt sticky. She had never been a good liar; never been even a vaguely adequate one.

'It didn't,' she admitted huskily.

'You chickened out?' Nigel guessed.

Jodi let out a sigh of relief; Nigel had just given her the perfect answer to her dilemma.

'I…I was tired and I started to have second thoughts. And—'

Before she could tell Nigel that she had decided to write to Leo Jefferson rather than speak with him her cousin had cut across her to say tolerantly, 'I thought you wouldn't go through with it. Never mind. Uncle Nigel has ridden to the rescue for you. My boss has invited me over to dinner tonight, and I've asked him if I can take you along with me. He'll be speaking to Leo Jefferson himself next week, and if you put your case to him I'm sure he'll incorporate the plight of the school into his own discussion.'

'Oh, Nigel, that's very kind of you, but I don't think…' Jodi began to demur. She just wasn't in the mood for a dinner party, and as for the idea of putting the school's case to Nigel's boss, who was the chief planning officer for the area, Jodi's opinion of her own credibility had been so undermined that she just didn't feel good enough about herself to do so.

Nigel, though, made it clear that he was not prepared to take no for an answer.

'You've got to come,' he insisted. 'Graham really does want to meet you. His grandson is one of your pupils, apparently, and he's a big fan of yours. The grandson, not Graham. Although...'

'Nigel, I can't go,' Jodi protested.

'Of course you can. You must. Think of your school,' he teased her before adding, 'I'm picking you up at half-past seven, and you'd better be ready.'

He had rung off before Jodi could protest any further.

Wearily Jodi studied the screen of her computer. She had spent most of the afternoon trying to compose a letter to send to Leo Jefferson. The headache she had woken up with had, thankfully, finally abated, but every time she tried to concentrate on what she was supposed to be doing a totally unwanted mental picture of Leo Jefferson kept forming inside her head. And it wasn't just his face that her memory was portraying to her in intimate detail, she acknowledged as she felt herself turning as pink as the cascading petunias in her next-door neighbour's window boxes. Mrs Fields, at eighty, was still a keen gardener, and as she had ruefully explained to Jodi she liked the strong, bright colours because she could see them.

Jodi's own lovingly planted boxes were a more subtle combination of soft greens, white and silver, the same silver as Leo Jefferson's sexy eyes.

Jodi's face flamed even hotter as she stared at her screen and realised that she had begun her letter, 'Dear Sexy Eyes'.

Quickly she deleted the words and began again, reminding herself of how important it was that she impress on Leo Jefferson the effect the closure of the factory would have not just on her school but also on the whole community.

All over the country small villages were dying or becoming weekend dormitories for city workers, although everyone here in their local community had worked hard to make theirs a living, working village.

If she could get Nigel's boss on her side it was bound to help their case. Frowning slightly, she pushed her chair away from her computer. She ought to be used to fighting to keep the school going now. When she had first been appointed as its head teacher she had been told by the education authority that it would only be for an interim period, as, with the school's numbers falling, it would ultimately have to be closed.

Even though she had known she would get better promotion and higher pay by transferring to a bigger school, as soon as Jodi had realised the effect that losing their school would have she had begun to canvass determinedly for new pupils, even to the extent of persuading parents who had previously been considering private education to give their local primary a chance.

Her efforts had paid off in more ways than one, and Jodi knew she would never forget the pride she had felt when their school had received an excellent report following an inspection visit.

Her pride wasn't so much for herself, though, as for the efforts of the pupils and everyone else who had supported the school; to have to stand back and see all the ground they had gained lost, the sense of teamwork and community she had so determinedly fostered amongst the pupils destroyed, was more than she wanted to have to bear.

She had proved just how well the children thrived and learned in an atmosphere of security and love, in a school where they were known and valued as individuals, and Jodi was convinced that the self-confidence such a start gave them was something that would benefit them through their academic lives. But somehow, trying to explain all of this to Leo Jefferson was far harder than she had expected.

Perhaps it was because she suspected that he had already made up his mind, that, so far as he was concerned, the small community he would be destroying simply didn't matter when compared with his profits. Or perhaps it was because all she could think about, all she could see, was last night and the way they had been together...

With every hour that distanced her from the intimacy they had shared it became harder for her to acknowledge what she had done. It just wasn't like her to behave in such a way, and the proof of that, had she needed any, was the fact that he, Leo Jefferson, had been her first and only lover!

Too overwrought to concentrate, Jodi stood up and started to pace the floor of her small sitting room in emotional agitation.

Shocking though her behaviour had been, she knew and could not deny that she had enjoyed Leo Jefferson's touch, his lovemaking, his possession.

But that was because she had been half-drunk and half-asleep, she tried to defend herself, before her strong sense of honesty ruthlessly reminded her of the way she had reacted to him when she had first seen him, when she had quite definitely been both sober and awake!

It was nearly six o'clock. Her letter wasn't finished, but she would have to leave it now and go and get ready for the evening.

Nigel was going to a lot of trouble on her behalf and she ought to feel grateful to him. Instead, all she wanted was to stay at home and hide from the world until she had come to terms with what she had done.

CHAPTER THREE

LEO grimaced as he ran a hand over his newly shaven jaw. There was no way he felt like going out to dinner, but when Graham Johnson, the chief planning officer for the area, had rung to invite him to his home Leo had not felt he could refuse.

It made good business sense to establish an amicable arrangement with the local authority. Leo had already met Graham and liked him, and when Graham had explained that there was someone he would find it interesting to meet on an informal basis Leo had sensed that Graham would not be very impressed were he to turn him down. And besides, at least if he went out it would stop him from thinking about last night, and that wretched, unforgettably sexy woman who had got so dangerously under his skin.

As yet, Jeremy Driscoll had made no attempt to contact him, and Leo was hoping that he had the sense to recognise that Leo was not to be coerced—in any way—but somehow he doubted that Jeremy had actually given up. He wasn't that type, and, since he had gone as far as paying his accomplice to play her part, Leo suspected that he was going to want value for his money.

Did Driscoll avail himself of Leo's tousle-haired tormentor's sexual skills? It shocked Leo to discover just how unpalatable he found that thought! Was he crazy, feeling possessive about a woman like that, a woman

43

any man could have? Unwantedly Leo found himself remembering the way her body had claimed him, tightening around him almost as though it had known no other man. Now he *was* going crazy, he told himself angrily as he peered at the approaching signpost to check that he was driving in the right direction.

'Jodi, you aren't listening to me.'

Jodi gave her cousin an apologetic look as he brought his car to a halt outside his boss's house.

'Come to think of it, you're not exactly looking your normal, chirpy self.' He gave her a concerned look. 'Worrying about that school of yours, I expect?'

Ignoring his question, Jodi drew a deep breath, determined to tackle him about an issue that had been weighing very heavily on her mind.

'Nigel, what on earth possessed you to order that cocktail for me last night? You know I don't drink, and because it never occurred to me that it was alcoholic…well, there was so much fruit in it…'

'Hey, hang on a minute,' Nigel protested in bewilderment. 'I never ordered you anything alcoholic.'

'Well, whatever the waiter brought to Leo Jefferson's suite definitely was,' Jodi informed him grittily.

'They must have misunderstood me,' Nigel told her. 'I asked them to send you up a fruit cocktail. I thought it seemed expensive—what a waste; I bet you didn't touch it after the first swallow, did you?'

Fortunately, before she was obliged to lie to him, he took hold of Jodi's arm and walked her firmly towards the front door, which opened as they reached it to reveal their host, Graham Johnson, a tall grey-haired man with a warm smile.

'You must be Jodi.' He shook Jodi's hand, and introduced himself. 'I've heard an awful lot about you!'

When Jodi gave Nigel a wry look their host shook his head and laughed.

'No, not from Nigel, although he has mentioned you. I was referring to our grandson, Henry. He's one of your pupils and an ardent admirer. With just reason, too, according to his parents. Our daughter, Charlotte, is most impressed with the dramatic improvement the school has achieved in Henry's reading skills.'

Jodi smiled her appreciation of his compliments and a little of the tension started to leave her body as they followed Graham into the house.

Mary Johnson was as welcoming as her husband, informing Jodi that she had trained as a teacher herself, although it had been many years since she had last taught.

'My daughter was a little concerned at first when she heard that you were an advocate of a mixture of traditional teaching methods and educational play, but she's a total convert now. She can't stop telling us how much Henry's spatial skills have improved along with his reading ability.'

'We like to encourage the children to become good all-rounders,' Jodi acknowledged, explaining, 'We feel that it helps overall morale if we can encourage every child to discover a field in which they can do well.'

'I understand from our daughter that you've actually got parents putting their children's names down for the school almost as soon as they are born.'

'Well, perhaps not quite that,' Jodi laughed, 'but certainly we are finding that our reputation has been spread by word of mouth. We're above the safety limit we need to satisfy the education authority as regards pupil numbers and likely to stay that way, unless, of course, the factory is closed down.'

Jodi gave Graham Johnson an uncertain look as she saw his expression.

'The final decision with regard to that rests with Leo Jefferson,' he told her gently, 'which is why I've invited him to join us for dinner tonight. It was Nigel's idea, and a good one. It might help matters if the two of you were to meet in an informal setting. I suspect that from a businessman's point of view Leo Jefferson hasn't really considered the effect a closure of the factory would have on the village school. And, of course, it isn't inevitable that he will close down our factory. As I understand it, of the four he has taken over he only intends to close two.'

Jodi wasn't really listening to him. She had stopped listening properly the moment he had said those dreadful words, 'I've invited him to join us for dinner tonight'.

Leo Jefferson was coming here. For dinner. She was going to be forced to sit in the same room with him, perhaps even across the table from him.

She felt sick, faint, paralysed with fear, she recognised as the doorbell rang and Graham went to answer it.

Frantically she looked at the French windows, aching to make her escape through them, but it was already too late, Graham was walking back into the room accompanied by Leo Jefferson. The man she had spent the night with... Her lover!

*　　*　　*

Leo had been listening politely to his host as Graham showed him the way to the sitting room, opened the door and ushered Leo inside. He proceeded to introduce Leo to the other occupants of the room, but the moment he had stepped through the door Leo stopped hearing a single word that Graham was saying as he stared in furious disbelief at Jodi.

She was standing by the French windows, looking for all the world like some martyr about to be taken away for beheading, her eyes huge with anguish and fear as she stared mutely at him.

What was going on? What was she doing here? And then Leo realised that Graham was introducing her to him as the local school's head teacher.

He felt as though he had somehow strayed into some kind of farce. He accepted that things were different in the country, but surely not so damned different that a village headmistress moonlighted as a professional harlot!

The surge of furious jealousy that burst over the banks of his normal self-control bewildered him, as did the immediate antipathy he felt towards the man standing at her side.

'And this is Nigel Marsh, my assistant and Jodi's cousin,' Graham Johnson was explaining.

Her cousin. To his own relief Leo felt himself easing back on his ridiculous emotions.

'A little surprise for you!' Nigel whispered to Jodi whilst Mary was talking to Leo.

Jodi gave him a wan smile.

'Jodi, can I get you a drink?' Graham was asking jovially.

'I don't usually drink, thank you,' Jodi responded automatically, and then flushed a deep, rich pink as she saw the look that Leo Jefferson was giving her.

'She's always been strait-laced, even before she qualified as a teacher,' Nigel informed Graham humorously. 'Can't think how we came to share the same gene pool. I'm always telling her that she ought to loosen up a little, enjoy life, let herself go.'

Jodi didn't want to look at Leo Jefferson again, but somehow she couldn't stop herself from doing so. To her shock he had moved closer to her, and whilst Nigel responded to something Mary was saying he leaned forward and whispered cynically to Jodi, 'That's quite a personality change you've managed to accomplish in less than twenty-four hours.'

'Please,' Jodi implored him, desperately afraid that he might be overheard, but to her relief the others had moved out of earshot.

'Please... I seem to remember you said something like that to me last night,' Leo reminded her silkily.

'Stop it,' Jodi begged in torment. 'You don't understand.'

'You're damned right I don't!' Leo agreed acerbically, adding, 'Tell me something; do your school governors know that you're moonlighting as a hooker? I accept that schoolteachers may not be overly well-paid, but somehow I've never imagined them supplementing their income with those sort of private lessons.'

'No, you...'

Jodi meant to continue and tell Leo he had it all wrong, but her vehement tone caused Nigel to break off his conversation with Mary Johnson and give her a concerned look. He knew how passionate she was about her school, but he hadn't expected to hear her arguing with Leo Jefferson so early in the evening. It did not augur well. However, before Nigel could step in with some diplomatic calming measures Mary was announcing that she was ready for them to sit down for dinner.

'That was absolutely delicious.' Nigel sighed appreciatively as he ate the last morsel of his pudding. 'Living on your own is all very well, but microwave meals can't take the place of home cooking. I keep saying as much to Jodi,' he continued plaintively to Mary, giving Jodi a teasing glance. 'But she doesn't seem to take the hint.'

'If you want home cooking you should learn to cook yourself,' Jodi returned firmly. 'I insist that all the children at school, boys and girls, learn the basics.'

'And I think it's wonderful that they do,' Mary supported her, turning to Leo to tell him, 'Jodi has done wonders for her school. When she first took over they had so few pupils that it was about to be closed down, but now parents are putting down their children's names at birth to ensure that they get a place.'

Jodi could feel herself starting to colour up as Leo turned to look at her.

The whole evening had been a nightmare, and so far as she was concerned it couldn't come to an end fast enough.

'Oh, yes, Jodi is passionate about her school,' Nigel chimed in supportively.

'Passionate?'

Jodi could feel the anxiety tensing her already over-stretched nervous system as Leo drawled the word with an undertone of cynical dislike that she hoped only she could hear. Was he going to give her away?

To her relief, Leo went on, 'Oh, yes, I'm sure she is.'

'I think,' Graham began to say calmly, with a kind smile in Jodi's direction, 'that she is also concerned about the potential effect if would have on the school if you were to close down the Frampton factory.'

When Leo gave him a sharp look Graham gave a small shrug and told him, 'It's no secret that you intend to close one and possibly two of the factories—the financial Press have quoted you on it.'

'It's a decision I haven't made as yet,' Leo responded tersely.

'So are you considering closing down our factory?' Jodi couldn't resist demanding.

Leo frowned as he listened to her. She had hardly spoken directly to him all night. In fact, she had barely even looked at him, but he could feel both her tension and her hostility as keenly as he could feel his own reaction to her.

It infuriated him, in a way that was a whole new experience for him, that she should be able to play so well and so deceitfully the role of a dedicated schoolteacher when he knew what she really was.

She must be completely without conscience! And she was in charge of the growth and development of burgeoning young minds and emotions. How clever she must be to be able to dupe everyone around her so successfully; to be able to win their trust and merit their admiration and respect.

Leo told himself that the intensity of his own emotions was a completely natural reaction to the discovery of her duplicity. If he was to reveal the truth about her—but, of course, he couldn't, after all he wasn't exactly proud of his own behaviour.

But why had she done it? For money, as he had originally assumed? Because she enjoyed flirting with danger? Because she wanted to help Driscoll? For some reason, it was this last option that he found the least palatable.

Jodi could feel Leo's bitterly contemptuous gaze burning the distance between them. If he should mention last night...! If Nigel had given her the slightest indication that Leo was going to be a fellow guest no power on earth would have been able to get her within a mile of Mary and Graham's.

She had cringed inwardly, listening to the others singing her praises, hardly daring to breathe in case Leo said anything. But of course last night's events did not reflect much more credibly on him than they did on her. Although he, as a man, at least had the age-old excuse of claiming, as so many of his sex had done throughout history, that the woman had tempted him.

Soon their current school term would be over. Normally she experienced a certain sadness when this happened, especially at the end of the summer term, since their eldest pupils would be moving on to 'big' school. Right now she felt she couldn't wait for the freedom to quietly disappear out of public view.

A couple of friends from university had invited her to join them on a walking holiday in the Andes and she wished that she had agreed to go with them. Instead, she had said she wanted to spend some time decorating her small house and working on her garden, as well as planning ways to make the school even better than it already was—something which in Jodi's eyes was more of a pleasure than a chore.

Now, thanks to Leo Jefferson, all the small pleasures she had been looking forward to had been obscured by the dark cloud of her own guilt.

'Well, we shall certainly be very disappointed if you choose to close down our factory,' she could hear Graham saying to Leo. 'We're a small country area and replacing so many lost jobs isn't going to be easy. Although logically I can understand that the Newham factory does have the advantage of being much closer to the motorway network.'

'Unfortunately, it is all a question of economics,' Leo was replying. 'The market simply isn't big enough to support so many different factories all producing the same thing...'

Suddenly Jodi had heard enough. Her passionate desire to protect her school overwhelmed the fear and shame that had kept her silent throughout the evening and, turning towards Leo, she told him angrily, 'It managed to support them well enough before your takeover, and it seems to me that it would be more truthful to say that the economics in question are those that affect your profits—not to mention the tax advantages you will no doubt stand to gain. Have you no idea of the hardship it's going to cause? The people it will put out of work, the lives and families it will destroy? I've got children at school whose whole family are dependent on that factory—fathers, mothers, grandparents, aunts, uncles. Don't you care about anything except making money?'

Jodi could feel the small, shocked silence her outburst had caused. Across the table, Nigel was giving her a warning look, whilst Graham Johnson was frowning slightly.

'We all understand how you feel, Jodi.' he told her calmly. 'But I'm afraid that economics, profits, can't just be ignored. Leo is competing in a worldwide marketplace, and for his business to remain successful—'

'There are far more important things in life than profits,' Jodi interrupted him, unable to stop herself from stemming the intensity of her feelings now that she had started to speak.

'Such as what?' Leo checked her sharply. 'Such as you keeping enough pupils in your school to impress the school inspectorate? Aren't you just as keen to show a profit on your pupil numbers in return for Education Authority funding as I am on my financial investment in my business?'

'How dare you say that?' Jodi breathed furiously. 'It is the children themselves, their education, their futures, their lives, that concern me. What you are doing—'

'What I am doing is trying to run a profitable business.' Leo silenced her acidly. 'You, I'm afraid, are blinkered by your own parochial outlook. I have to see the bigger picture. If I was to keep all the factories operating inevitably none of them would be profitable and I would then be out of business, with the loss of far more jobs than there will be if I simply close down two of them.'

'You just don't care, do you?' Jodi challenged him.

'You don't care about what you're doing; about the misery you will be causing.'

She knew that she was going too far, and that both Nigel and the Johnsons were watching her with concern and dismay, but something was driving her on. The tension she had been feeling all evening had somehow overwhelmed the rational parts of her brain and she was in the hands of a self-destructive, unstoppable urge she couldn't control.

'What I care about is keeping my business at the top of its field,' Leo told her grimly.

'Precisely,' Jodi threw at him, curling her lip in contempt as she tossed her head. 'Profit… Don't you care that what you are doing is totally immoral?'

Jodi tensed as she heard the sharp hiss of collective indrawn breath as she and Leo confronted one another in bitter hostility.

'*You* dare to accuse me of immorality!'

Had the others heard, as she had, the way he had emphasised the word 'you'? Jodi wondered in sick shock as she tried to withstand the icy contempt of the look he was giving her.

'Jodi, my dear.' Graham finally intervened a little uncomfortably. 'I'm sure we all appreciate how strongly you feel about everything, but Leo does have a point. Naturally his business has to be competitive.'

'Oh, naturally,' Jodi agreed bitingly, throwing Leo a caustic look.

Nigel was standing up, saying that it was time that they left, but as Graham pulled out Jodi's chair for her she still couldn't resist turning to Leo to challenge, 'In the end everything comes down to money, doesn't it?'

As he, too, stood up he looked straight at her and told her softly, 'As you should know.'

Jodi could feel her face burning.

'Oh, and by the way,' Leo added under cover of Mary going to fetch them all their coats, 'you can tell your friend Driscoll—'

Jodi didn't let him get any further.

'Jeremy Driscoll is no friend of mine,' she told him immediately. 'In fact, if you want the truth, I loathe and detest him almost as much as I do you.'

She was shaking as she thanked Mary and slipped on her coat, hurrying out into the warmth of the summer night ahead of Nigel, who had turned back to say something to their host.

As she waited for him beside the car, her back towards the house, she was seething with anger. At the same time she began to feel the effects of the shock of seeing Leo Jefferson and the way she had argued with him so publicly.

As she heard Nigel come crunching over the gravel towards her, without turning to look at him, she begged fiercely, 'Just take me out of here...'

'Where exactly is it you want me to take you? Or can I guess?'

Whirling round, Jodi expelled her breath on a hissing gasp as she realised that it wasn't Nigel who was standing next to her in the shadow of the trees but Leo Jefferson.

'Keep away from me,' she warned him furiously, inadvertently backing into the shadows as she strove to put more distance between them.

Her reaction, so totally overplayed and unwarranted, was the last straw so far as Leo was concerned.

'Oh, come on,' he snarled. 'You haven't got an audience now!'

'You don't know anything,' Jodi spat back shakily.

'That wasn't what you were telling me last night,' Leo couldn't stop himself from reminding her savagely. 'Last night—'

'Last night I didn't know what I was doing,' Jodi retaliated bitterly. 'If I had done I would never…' She was so overwrought now that her voice and her body both trembled. 'You are the last man I would have wanted to share what should have been one of the most special experiences of my life.'

Jodi was beyond thinking logically about what she was revealing; instead she was carried along, flung headlong into the powerful vortex of her own overwhelming emotions.

Leo could hear what she was saying, but, like her, his emotions were too savagely aroused for him to take on board the meaning of her words. Instead he held out to her the handbag she had unknowingly left behind in the house, telling her coldly, 'You forgot this. Your cousin is still talking with Graham and Mary and he asked me to bring it to you. I think he probably wanted to give you the opportunity to apologise to me in private for your appalling rudeness over dinner…'

'*My* rudeness.' Jodi reached angrily for her handbag and then froze as her fingertips brushed against Leo's outstretched hand.

Just the feel of his skin against her own sent a shower

of sharp electric shocks, of unwanted sensation, slicing through her body.

'Don't touch me,' she protested, and then moaned a soft, tormented sound of helpless need, dropping her handbag and swaying towards him in exactly the same breath as he reached for her. He dragged her against his body and the feel of him was so savagely, shockingly familiar that her body reacted instantly. She looked up into his face, her lips parting. His mouth burned against hers like a brand, punishing, taking, possessing. She felt him shudder as his fingers bit into the tender flesh of her upper arms. But then as his tongue-tip probed her lips he seemed to change his mind. He released her abruptly and, turning on his heel, walked away.

It was several seconds before she could stop shaking enough to bend down and pick up her bag. Whilst she was doing so she heard Nigel saying her name.

'Sorry about the delay,' he apologised as she stood up and he unlocked the car. 'Feeling better now that you've got all that off your chest?' he asked her wryly.

'Better?' Jodi demanded sharply as they both got into his car. 'How could I possibly be feeling better after having to spend an evening with that…that…?'

'OK, OK, I get the picture,' Nigel told her, adding, 'In fact, I think we all did. I do understand how you feel, Jodi, but ripping up at Leo Jefferson isn't going to help. He's a businessman and you've got to try to see things from his point of view.'

'Why should I see things from his point of view? He doesn't seem to be prepared to see them from mine,' Jodi challenged her cousin.

Nigel gave her a wry look.

'There is a very apt saying about catching more flies with honey than vinegar,' he reminded her, 'although something tells me you aren't in the mood to hear that.'

Jodi could feel her face starting to burn.

'No, I'm not,' she said tersely.

'Why couldn't things have just stayed the way they were?' she moaned to Nigel as he drove her home. 'Everything was all right when the Driscolls owned the factory.'

'Not totally,' Nigel told her quietly, but shook his head when Jodi looked at him. He had already said too much, and he wasn't yet free to tell her about the fraudulent practices that Jeremy Driscoll was suspected of having operated within the business.

Jodi didn't push him further on that point; instead she burst out, 'Leo Jefferson is the most hateful, horrid, arrogant, impossible man I have ever met and I wish...I wish...'

Unable to specify just exactly what she wished, and why, Jodi bit her lip and looked out of the car window, glad to see that they were already in the village and that she would soon be home.

Leo grimaced as he paced the sitting-room floor of his suite. He had a good mind to ring down to Reception and ask them to transfer him to a different set of rooms; these reminded him too much of last night and her— Jodi Marsh!

That infuriating woman who had by some alchemic means turned herself from the wanton, sensual creature who had shared his bed last night into the furious, spiky opponent who had had the gall tonight to sit there and accuse *him* of immoral behaviour! How he had stopped himself from challenging her there and then to justify herself Leo really didn't know. And she was a schoolteacher! Perhaps he was being unduly naïve, but he just couldn't get his head around it at all.

And as for her comments about his plans for the factory and the effect it would have on other people's lives if he was to close it down…!

Leo frowned. Did she think he enjoyed having to put people out of work? Of course he didn't, but economic factors were economic factors and could not simply be ignored.

Well, he just hoped that she didn't get it into her head to come back tonight and pay him a second visit, because if she did she would find there was no way he was going to be as idiotically vulnerable to her as he had been last night. No way at all!

CHAPTER FOUR

'YOU pushed me.'

'No, I didn't.'

With gentle firmness Jodi sorted out the dispute caused by one of her most problematic pupils on her way across the school yard.

Left to his own devices, she suspected, seven-year-old Ben Fanshawe might have been a happy, sociable child, but, thanks to the efforts of his social-climbing mother, Ben was a little boy with an attitude that was driving the other children away.

Jodi had tried tactfully to discuss the situation with his mother, but Ben's problems were compounded by the fact that Myra Fanshawe was not just a parent, but also on the school's board of governors. It was a position she had single-mindedly set her sights on from the minute she and her husband had moved into the village.

A close friend of Jeremy Driscoll and his wife, Myra had made it plain to Jodi that she would have preferred to send her son to an exclusive prep school. It was only because her in-laws were refusing to pay their grandson's school fees until he was old enough to attend the same school as the previous six generations of male Fanshawes that Ben was having to attend the village primary school.

Having bullied and badgered her way into the position of Chair of the Board of Governors, Myra had continually bombarded both the board and Jodi herself with her opinions on how the school might be improved.

Having lost her most recent battle to impose a system of teaching maths that she had decided would be enormously beneficial for Ben, Myra had made it abundantly clear to Jodi that she had made a bad enemy.

For Ben's sake, Jodi had tried tactfully to suggest that he might benefit from being encouraged to make more friends amongst his schoolmates. But her gentle hints had been met with fury and hostility by Myra, who had told Jodi that there was no way she wanted her son mixing with 'common village children'.

'Once Benjamin leaves here he will be meeting a very different class of child. He already knows that, and knows too that I would have preferred him to be attending a proper prep school. I do wish I could make his grandparents understand how much better it would be if he was already in private education. Jeremy and Alison were totally appalled that we could even think of allowing him to come here. At least now that I'm Chair of the Board of Governors I shall be able to make sure that he is receiving the rudiments of a decent education.

'The vicar's wife commented to me only the other day how much better the school has been doing since I became involved.' She had preened herself, leaving Jodi torn between pity for her little boy and amazement at Myra's total lack of awareness of other people's feelings.

As it happened, Anna Leslie, the vicar's wife, had actually told Jodi herself how unbearable she found Myra and how much she loathed her patronising attitude.

With only such a short time to go before the end of term, it was perhaps only natural that the children should be in such a high-spirited mood, Jodi acknowledged as she made her way to her office.

By the time the school bell rang to summon the children to their classes she was so engrossed in her work that she had almost managed to put Leo Jefferson right out of her mind.

Almost…

Leo tensed as his mobile phone rang. He was in his car, on his way to meet with his accountant at the Frampton factory that had been the subject of his heated exchange of views with Jodi on Saturday night.

He frowned as he registered the unavailable number of his caller. If Jodi was ringing him in an attempt to… Reaching out, he answered the call using the car's hands-free unit, but the voice speaking his name was not Jodi's and was not, in fact, even female, but belonged instead to Jeremy Driscoll.

'Look, old boy, I just thought I'd give you a ring to see if the two of us couldn't get together. The word is that you're going to have to close down at least a couple of the factories and I'm prepared to make you a good offer to buy Frampton back from you.'

Leo frowned as he listened.

'Buy it?' he challenged him curtly, waiting for Jeremy to threaten to blackmail him into agreeing, but, to his surprise, Jeremy made no reference whatsoever to either Jodi or her visit to his bed.

'Look, we're both businessmen—and we both know there are ways and means of you selling the business back to me that would benefit us both financially…'

Leo didn't respond.

Jeremy Driscoll had been away on holiday in the Caribbean with his wife when his father-in-law had accepted Leo's offer to buy out the business, and it was becoming increasingly obvious to Leo that for some reason he did not wish to see the sale go through.

'I haven't made my mind up which factories I intend to close as yet,' Leo informed him. It was, after all, the truth.

'Frampton is the obvious choice. Anyone can see that,' Jeremy Driscoll was insisting. Beneath the hectoring tone of his voice Leo could hear a sharper note of anxiety.

Leo had almost reached the factory. Reaching out to end the call, he told Jeremy Driscoll crisply, 'I'll call you once I've made up my mind.'

As he cancelled the call Leo's frown deepened. It disturbed him that Jeremy Driscoll hadn't said a single word about Jodi. Somehow that seemed out of character. Driscoll wasn't the sort of man to miss an opportunity to maximise on his advantage and, even though Leo knew he wouldn't allow himself to be blackmailed, he was still in a potentially vulnerable position.

But nowhere near as delicate and vulnerable as the one Jodi herself was in, he acknowledged grimly. What on earth had possessed her?

'So what you're saying is that I should close this factory down?' Leo asked his accountant as they finished their tour of the Frampton site.

'Well, it does seem to be the obvious choice. Newham has the benefit of being much closer to the motorway system.'

'Which means that it would be relatively easy to sell off as a base for a haulage contractor,' Leo interrupted him wryly. 'That would then allow me to consolidate production at Frampton, and use the Newham site solely for distribution, or if that proved to be uneconomical to sell it off.'

'Well, yes, that could be an option,' the accountant acknowledged.

'Frampton also has the benefit of having recently had a new production line,' Leo continued.

'Yes, I know. It seems there was a fire, that destroyed the old one, which brings me to something else,' the accountant told him carefully. 'There are one or two things here that just don't tie up.'

'Such as?' Leo challenged him curiously.

'Such as two fires in a very short space of time, and certain anomalies in the accounting system. It seems that this factory has been run by the owners' son-in-law, who prior to working in the business gained a reputation for favouring practices which, shall we say, are not entirely in line with those approved of by the revenue.'

'So what we are actually talking about here is fraud,' Leo stated sharply.

'I don't know, and certainly I haven't found anything fraudulent in the accounts that were submitted to us on takeover. However, it may be that those accounts are not the only ones the business produced. Just call it a gut feeling, but something tells me that things are not totally as they should be.'

Had his accountant unwittingly hit on the reason why Jeremy Driscoll was so anxious to retain ownership of this particular factory? Leo wondered.

'If you're serious about finding a haulier buyer for the Newham land,' his accountant continued, 'I might know of someone.'

Leo stopped him. 'I might well opt to set up my own distribution network. With distribution costs rising the way they are, it makes good economic sense to be able to control that aspect of the business.'

'Mmm…'

What the hell was he doing? Leo asked himself in inner exasperation. He was finding arguments to keep Frampton open! Surely he wasn't allowing himself to be influenced by the emotional opinions of a woman who knew nothing about business? Although she did know everything about how to please a man. This man! How to infuriate and drive him insane was more like it, Leo decided in furious, angry rejection of his own weak thoughts.

He and the accountant parted company at the factory gate. It was almost lunchtime, and Leo recalled that there was a pub in the village where he could no doubt get something to eat.

If he was to change his plans and retain the Frampton factory it would mean spending a good deal of time in the area; several months at least. He would have to rent somewhere to live.

Perhaps predictably the pub was almost opposite the church, and separated from the church by the graveyard and a small paddock was the school.

Her school!

Since it was lunchtime, the school yard was filled with children.

Turning into the pub car park, Leo parked and then

got out to walk round to the main entrance to the dining room.

As he did so his attention was caught by a small group of children clustering around a familiar figure.

Jodi's curls were burnished a deep, rich colour by the sunlight. She was wearing a cotton skirt and a toning blouse, her legs bare beneath the hem of her skirt.

She hadn't seen him, Leo acknowledged, and she was laughing at something one of her pupils had said, her head thrown back to reveal the taut line of her throat, with its creamy smooth skin, the same skin he had caressed and kissed.

Leo could feel the sensual reaction filling his body. He still wanted her!

She looked completely at home in her chosen role and Leo could see that the children were equally relaxed with her. And then, as though somehow she had sensed his presence, she looked towards him, her whole body freezing and the joy dying abruptly from her face as their gazes battled silently across the distance that separated them.

As though they sensed her hostility the children too had become still and silent, and as he watched Leo saw her ushering them away from the school boundary out of sight.

The pub dining room was surprisingly busy, but Leo barely paid any attention to his fellow diners. His thoughts were taken up with Jodi, a fact which caused him to wonder grimly yet again just what the hell was happening to him.

He ate his meal quickly without really being aware of

it. In his mind's eye he could still see Jodi surrounded by her pupils. She had looked…

He shook his head, trying to dismiss her image from his thoughts, and caused the waitress who had served him to give a tiny little shiver and reflect on how dangerous and exciting he looked—and how very different from her boyfriend!

Having finished his meal and refused a second cup of coffee, much to the waitress's secret disappointment, Leo got up, oblivious to her interest in him.

On his way back to the car he noticed that the school playground was now empty, the children no doubt back at their desks.

For God's sake, he derided himself as he drove back towards the town, didn't he have enough to think about at the moment without being obsessed by a schoolteacher?

'Well, we don't normally have many rental properties,' the agent in the local town was informing Leo. 'But it just so happens that we've been asked to find a tenant for a thoroughly charming Georgian house, just outside Frampton. I don't know if you know the village.'

'Yes, I know it,' Leo confirmed a little grimly.

'I live there myself.' The agent smiled. 'I don't know if you have children, but if you do I can thoroughly recommend the village school. Jodi Marsh, the head teacher, is wonderful—'

'I know Jodi,' Leo interrupted him brusquely.

'You do?' The agent gave him a discreetly speculative look. 'Well, if you're a friend of Jodi's you'll find you get a very warm welcome in the village. She's as popular with the parents as she is with the children, and deservedly so.

'My wife dreads the thought of her leaving; she says the school just wouldn't be the same without her. We all admire the way she campaigned so tirelessly to keep the school open and to raise enough money to buy the playing field adjacent to it to stop Jeremy Driscoll from acquiring it as building land. That didn't make her popular with Jeremy at all, but Jodi has never been a fan of his, as you'll probably know…'

Again he gave Leo a speculative look, but Leo discovered that he was strangely reluctant to correct the other man's misconceptions. For one thing he was too busy analysing the agent's surprising comments about Jodi's antipathy towards Jeremy Driscoll to notice.

'If you'd like to view Ashton House?' the agent continued questioningly.

Leo told himself that he should refuse, that deliberately choosing to live anywhere within a hundred-mile radius of Jodi Marsh was complete madness, but for some reason he heard himself agreeing to see the house, and accepting the agent's suggestion that they should drive over to view it immediately.

'I rather get the impression that Jeremy Driscoll isn't the most popular of people around here?' Leo commented to the agent half an hour later as they stood together in front of the pretty Georgian property.

'Well, no, he isn't,' the agent agreed. 'And, despite the fact that he's married, Jeremy fancies himself as something of a ladies' man. Of course Jodi, in particular, is well known for her strict moral code, so I suppose it was almost inevitable that she should make it very plain to him that his advances were unwelcome.'

Leo struggled to absorb this new information as the agent changed tack to tell him about the house. 'It was built originally for the younger son of a local landowner; it's listed, of course, and with all its original internal decorative features—a real gem. If I had the money I would be very tempted to put in an offer for it. The elderly lady who owned it died a few weeks ago, and the beneficiaries under her will ultimately want to sell it, but until the estate is sorted out they need to find a tenant for it so that it doesn't fall into disrepair. Shall we go inside?'

The house was undoubtedly, as the agent had said, a 'gem', and had he been looking for a permanent home Leo knew that he too would have been tempted to acquire it. As it was, he was more than happy to meet the relatively modest rent the owners were requesting.

However, as Leo followed the agent back to his office, so that they could complete the paperwork for the rental, it wasn't so much the new temporary home he had acquired that was occupying his thoughts as the agent's revelations about Jodi.

Just why was it that everyone seemed to think that Jodi was a paragon of all the virtues? There was no way that he could be wrong about her, was there?

But later on in the day as he drove back to his hotel he was aware of a small and very unwanted niggling doubt that somehow just would not be silenced. Was it realistic for him to believe that so many other people were wrong and that he was right? Common sense told him that it wasn't!

But nothing changed the fact that Jodi had still, most definitely, been in his bed!

Jodi forced herself to smile at the group of fathers gathered in a huddle outside the school gates, talking to one another whilst they kept a protective eye on their children.

The factory operated a shift system, which meant that quite a large proportion of the families where both parents worked split the task of delivering and collecting their offspring from school. Fathers for some reason seemed to favour afternoon school runs, and if Jodi hadn't still been preoccupied with her thoughts of Leo Jefferson she would have stopped for a chat.

As it was, whilst walking past she registered the fact that the men were discussing the possible closure of the factory, and how they intended to make their objections known.

'We should do something to stop the closure!' someone protested angrily. 'We can't just stand by and lose our jobs, our livelihood.'

'What we need to do is to stage a demonstration,' another man was insisting.

A demonstration! Well, Jodi couldn't blame them for wanting to make their feelings public; she would be tempted to do exactly the same thing if anyone was to threaten to close her beloved school.

A tiny frown creased her forehead. These parents were the very ones who had supported her unstintingly in her determination to keep the school open, and in her fundraising to make sure that the school retained its adjacent playing field. The very least she could do, surely, was to support them in turn now. And her feelings about Leo Jefferson had nothing to do with it...

Retracing her footsteps, she walked back towards the small group.

'I couldn't help overhearing what you were just saying about demonstrating against the closure of the factory,' she began. 'If you do—' she took a deep breath '—you can certainly count on my support.'

'What, publicly?' one of them challenged her.

'Publicly!' Jodi confirmed firmly. As she spoke she had the clearest mental image of Leo Jefferson, watching her with icy-eyed contempt across Mary and Graham's dinner-table...

'Leo... Have you got a moment?'

Halfway across the hotel foyer, Leo stopped as Nigel Marsh came hurrying towards him.

'Look, I was wondering if we might have a word?'

Leo frowned as he looked at Jodi's cousin. The younger man looked both slightly uncomfortable and at the same time very determined.

Shooting back the cuff of his jacket, Leo glanced at his watch before telling him crisply, 'I can give you ten minutes.'

Nigel looked relieved.

'Thanks. I just wanted to have a word with you about Jodi...my cousin...you met her the other evening.'

He was speaking as though Leo might have forgotten just who Jodi was, Leo recognised, wondering just what Nigel Marsh would say if Leo was to tell him that Jodi was someone he would never be able to forget.

However, Leo had no intention of revealing any such

thing. Instead he replied with dry irony, 'You mean the schoolteacher.'

Nigel gave him a relieved look.

'Yes. Look, I know she must have come across to you as…as having a bit of a bee in her bonnet about your takeover—'

'She certainly has plenty of attitude,' Leo cut in coolly, causing Nigel to check himself. 'And a very hostile attitude where I'm concerned,' Leo continued crisply.

'It isn't anything personal,' Nigel denied immediately. 'It's just that the school means so much to her. She's worked damned hard to make it successful, and she's always been the kind of person who is attracted to lame dogs, lost causes… I remember when we were kids, she was always mothering something or someone. I know she went a little bit over-the-top the other night. But she wasn't expecting to see you there, and I suppose having hyped herself up to put her case to you at the hotel the night before and then having chickened out…'

He stopped suddenly, looking uncomfortably self-conscious, realising that he had said more than he should, but it was too late; Leo was already demanding sharply, 'Would you mind explaining that last comment, please?'

Even more uncomfortably Nigel did as he had been requested.

Leo waited until he had finished before asking him incredulously, 'You're saying that Jodi, your cousin, planned to approach me in person in my suite so that she could put the school's position to me and ask me to reconsider closing down the factory?'

'I know that technically I shouldn't have encouraged or helped her,' Nigel acknowledged, 'and Graham will probably read me the Riot Act if he finds out, but I just couldn't not do something. If you really knew her you'd understand that.'

Leo did, and he understood a hell of a lot more now too. Like just why Jodi had been in his room. His room, but not his bed! Had she ordered that nauseating alcoholic concoction to give herself some false courage? And then perhaps over-indulged in it? If so…

Nigel was still speaking and he forced himself to listen to what he was saying.

'Jodi deserves a break. She's battled so hard for the school. First to improve the teaching standards enough to get in more pupils, and then more recently against Jeremy Driscoll, to prevent him from acquiring the school's playing field.'

'I'd heard something about that,' Leo acknowledged.

'Jeremy wasn't at all pleased about the fact that he lost that piece of land. And, as I've already warned Jodi, she's made a dangerous enemy in him. It's no secret that he isn't at all well-liked locally.' Nigel gave a small grimace of distaste. 'Jodi can't stand him and I don't blame her.'

Leo started to frown, silently digesting what he was hearing. Nigel Marsh was the second person to tell him that Jodi didn't like Jeremy Driscoll.

Which meant…which meant that he had—perhaps—misjudged her on two counts. Yes, but that didn't explain away her extraordinary sensuality towards him in bed.

If he was to accept everyone else's opinion, such behaviour was totally out of character. As was his own, Leo was forced to acknowledge.

'I know that Jodi went a bit too far the other night,' Nigel was continuing, 'But in her defence I feel I have to say that she does have a point; without the factory—'

'Her precious school would be in danger of being closed down,' Leo interjected for him.

'We're a rural area, and it would be very hard to replace so many lost jobs,' Nigel said. 'That would mean that for people to find work they would have to move away, and so yes, ultimately the school could potentially be reduced to the position it was in when Jodi took over. But she's the kind of person who has always been sensitive to the feelings of others, and it is her concern for them that is motivating her far more than any concern she might have for her own career.'

He gave Leo a wry look.

'As a matter of fact, I happen to know that she's already been approached by a private school who are willing to pay her very well to go to them, and to include a package of perks that would include free education for her children were she to have any.'

'She isn't involved in a relationship with anyone, though, is she?' Leo couldn't stop himself from asking.

Fortunately Nigel did not seem to find anything odd in Leo's sudden question, shaking his head and informing him openly, 'Oh, no. She's one very picky lady, is my cousin. Casual relationships are just not her style, and as yet she hasn't met anyone she wants to become seriously involved with.'

'A career woman?' Leo hazarded.

'Well, she certainly loves her work,' Nigel conceded,

then changed the subject to tell Leo apologetically, 'Look, I've taken up enough of your time. I hope you don't mind me bending your ear on Jodi's behalf.'

'I'm half-Italian,' Leo responded with a brief shrug. 'Family loyalty is part of my heritage.'

It was the truth, and if he was honest Leo knew he would have to admit that he admired Nigel Marsh for his spirited defence of his cousin. But their conversation had left Leo with some questions only one person could answer—Jodi herself. But would she answer them? And would it really be wise of him to ask them and to risk becoming more involved with her?

More involved? Just how much more involved was it possible for two people to actually be? Leo wondered ironically.

Jodi closed her eyes and took a deep breath, filling her lungs with the soft, warm evening air. It was three days since she had last seen Leo Jefferson but he had never been far from her thoughts, even when she should, by rights, have been concentrating on other things. The committee meeting for the school's sports day, which she had attended two nights ago, for instance, and the impromptu and far less organised meeting she had attended last night to discuss the proposed demonstration outside the factory.

Feelings were running very high indeed with regard to the possible closure and, although Jodi had spoken to Nigel about it, he had not been able to tell her anything.

'Leo Jefferson has been in London, tied up in various meetings,' he had explained to her.

What he couldn't tell her, for professional reasons,

was that they had been informed there was a very real possibility that Jeremy Driscoll was going to be investigated with regard to anomalies in the stock records and accounts. It seemed there were considerable discrepancies involved for which no rational explanation had as yet been forthcoming.

Nigel had heard on the grapevine that Jeremy Driscoll was claiming the discrepancies had been caused by employee theft, and it was true that he had made insurance claims for such losses. However, the authorities were by no means convinced by his explanation, and it seemed that Leo Jefferson too was now questioning the validity of the accounts he had been provided with prior to buying the business.

Overhead, as Jodi climbed the narrow footpath that led to one of her favourite places, Ashton House—the beautiful Georgian manor house set in its own grounds outside the village—she could hear a blackbird trilling.

It had been agreed at last night's meeting that the workforce would start the demonstration tomorrow morning. Jodi was planning to join the demonstrators after school had finished for the day. As a student she had done her fair share of demonstrating, for both human- and animal-rights groups, and then, as now, as she had firmly explained to the committee, she was vehemently opposed to any kind of violence being used.

'I think we're all agreed on that point,' one of the mothers of Jodi's pupils had confirmed. 'I just wish it didn't have to come to this. We've tried to initiate talks with this Leo Jefferson, but he says that he doesn't consider it appropriate to meet with us at the moment.'

Leo!

Jodi closed her eyes and released her breath on a sigh.

She might not have seen him for three days, but that did not mean… Hastily she opened her eyes. She wasn't going to think about those dreams she kept on having night after night, or what they might mean. Dreams in which she was back in his hotel suite…his bed…his arms. They were just dreams, that was all. They didn't mean that she wanted a repetition of what had happened between them. The fact that she had woken up last night just in time to hear herself moaning his name meant nothing at all…and neither did the shockingly physical ache that seemed to be constantly tormenting her body whenever she forgot to control it.

And as for those shockingly savage kisses she kept dreaming about… Well, those just had to be a product of her own fevered imagination, didn't they?

CHAPTER FIVE

LEO frowned as he heard the sound of someone walking along the footpath that skirted round the boundary to Ashton House. He had moved in officially that morning, having organised a cleaning team to go through the house ahead of him. He was now exploring the garden and coming to the conclusion that it was going to take a dedicated team of gardeners to restore it to anything like its former glory.

He had spent the last few days in London, locked in a variety of meetings concerning both his acquisition of the factories and their future. And now it seemed the authorities wanted to open enquiries into the financial workings of the Frampton factory, in particular whilst it had been under Jeremy Driscoll's management.

If he did decide to keep the factory going he would first of all need to make a decision about what to do with the other sites.

One of them housed the oldest factory, with an out-of-date production line and a depleted workforce, and was a natural choice to be closed down.

Of the other three…if he opted to keep Frampton in production he would have to either sell off the factory adjacent to the motorway system or change its usage to that of a distribution unit.

If he did that… Leo tensed as the walker drew level

with the gate in his walled garden that gave on to the path, and he had a clear view of her.

Jodi Marsh!

Jodi saw Leo at exactly the same time as he saw her. The sight of him froze her in her tracks. What was Leo Jefferson doing in the garden of Ashton House? Her house. The house she had secretly wanted from the first minute she had seen it!

Before she could gather herself together and hurry past he was opening the gate and coming towards her. He stood in front of her, blocking her path.

'I'd like to talk to you,' she heard him telling her coolly.

Jodi glared at him, praying that he couldn't hear the furious, racing thud of her heart or guess just what kind of effect he was having on her.

'Well, I certainly would not like to talk to you,' she retaliated.

Liar. Liar! her conscience tormented her silently. And you don't just want to talk to him either...

Horrified that he might somehow sense what she was feeling, Jodi tried to walk away, but he had already masterfully taken hold of her arm, and as she battled against the dizzying sensation of his touch somehow or other she found that she was being gently but firmly propelled through the gate and into the garden beyond.

She had been in the garden before—at the invitation of the old lady who had lived there who, like Leo, had happened to see her on the path one day.

She had ached then with sadness to see its neglect, and longed to be the one to restore both it and the house to their former glory. Of course that was an impossible dream. Jodi dreaded to imagine just how much money it would take to restore such a large house and so overgrown a garden. Far too much for her, but not, it seemed, too much for Leo Jefferson.

'Will you please stop manhandling me?' she demanded angrily as Leo closed the gate, and then her face burned a deep, betraying pink as she saw the way he was looking at her.

If he dared to say one word about anything she might have said to him under the influence of alcohol and desire she would... But to her relief he simply looked at her for several heart-stopping seconds before asking her quietly, 'What were you doing in my suite?'

Jodi gaped at him. It took her several precious moments to recover from the directness of his question, but finally she did so, rallying admirably to remind him firmly, 'Well, according to you, I was there because...' She stopped as he started to shake his head.

'I don't want you to tell me what I believed you were doing there, Jodi, I want to hear your version of events.'

Her version. Now he had surprised her. Stubbornly she looked away from him.

'It doesn't matter now, does it?' she challenged him.

'Doesn't it? According to your cousin, you were there to ask me to reconsider closing down the factory.'

Flustered, Jodi looked at him before demanding worriedly, 'You've been speaking to Nigel?'

Leo could tell that he had caught her off guard.

'I told him right from the start that it was a crazy idea, but he wouldn't listen.' Barely pausing for breath, she continued, 'I thought at first he meant that I should talk to you in the hotel foyer, but then he told me that he'd managed to borrow a key card.'

'And so you went up to the suite to wait for me and whilst you were there you ordered yourself a drink,' Leo supplied helpfully.

Jodi stared at him.

'No,' she denied vehemently, so vehemently that Leo knew immediately she was speaking the truth. Shaking her head, she told him angrily, 'I would never have ordered a drink without paying for it. No, I asked Nigel to arrange it for me. Nigel thought he'd ordered a soft drink, not—' She stopped abruptly, clamping her lips together and glowering at Leo.

'I can't see what possible relevance any of this has now,' she began, but Leo was determined to establish exactly what had happened—and why!

'So whilst you were waiting for me you drank the fruit punch, which was alcoholic, and then...'

Jodi had had enough.

'I don't want to talk about it,' she told him fiercely, 'and you can't make me.'

'You went to bed with me,' Leo reminded her softly. 'And from what I've learned about you, Jodi Marsh, that is something—'

'It was nothing,' Jodi denied sharply. 'And, anyway, you were the one who went to bed with me. I was already there, asleep.'

'In my bed...and you—' Leo stopped abruptly. This wasn't getting them anywhere and it wasn't what he wanted to say.

'Look,' he told her quietly, 'it seems that I misjudged the situation...made an error about the reasons for you being there,' he corrected himself. 'And, that being the case, I really think that we should discuss—'

'There isn't anything I want or need to discuss with you,' Jodi jumped in tensely.

The fact that he might have mistaken her reason for being in his suite, and even the fact that he was prepared to acknowledge as much, made no difference to what she had done or how she felt about it.

'What happened just isn't important enough to warrant discussing,' she added, determined to bring their conversation to an end, but to her consternation Leo was refusing to let the subject drop.

'Maybe not to you, but I happen to feel rather differently,' he said curtly. 'It is not, let me tell you, my habit to indulge in casual sex with a succession of unknown partners.'

Casual sex! Jodi had to struggle to prevent herself from physically cringing. Was there to be no end to the humiliation her behaviour was forcing her to suffer?

Before she could stop herself she was retorting passionately, 'For your information, I have not had a succession of partners, and in fact...'

Abruptly she fell silent, her face flushing. No, she must not tell him that! If she did he was bound to start asking even more questions than he already had, and there was absolutely no way she was going to tell him about that idiotic foolishness she had experienced when she had first seen him in the hotel foyer.

No doubt some might claim that she had fallen in love with him at first sight, and that was why...but she, Jodi, was made of sterner and far more realistic stuff. She was a modern-thinking woman and would not contemplate such nonsense!

What was it about her that infuriated him to the point where he itched to take hold of her and make her listen to him? Leo wondered distractedly, unable to stop himself from focusing on her mouth and remembering how hot and sweet it had tasted. He wanted to kiss her again now, right here. But she was already turning back towards the gate, and a sudden surge of common sense warned him against the folly of going after her and begging her to stay when it so plainly wasn't what she wanted. But she had wanted him that night. She had wanted him and he had wanted her right back. And for him the problem was that he still did.

'Jodi?' he began, making a last attempt to talk to her, but, as he had already known she would, she shook her head.

'No, I...'

She barely had time to give a disbelieving and indignant gasp before she was dragged unceremoniously and ruthlessly into Leo's arms, and held there tightly.

Against his ardent seeking mouth she tried to make a protest, but it was smothered immediately by the hot passion of his kiss...dizzying her, bemusing her, confusing her, so that somehow instead of repudiating him she was actually moving closer, reaching out to him...

Somewhere deep in her brain a warning bell started to ring, but Jodi ignored it, Leo was kissing her and there was no way she wanted anything, least of all some silly old warning bell, to come between her and the sheer intensity and excitement, the total bliss, of feeling his mouth moving possessively and passionately against her own.

'Mmm…'

Leo could feel the heavy, crazy thud of his heartbeat as Jodi suddenly dropped her defensive attitude and became so soft, so pliable, so bewitchingly and adorably warm in his arms that he was sorely tempted to pick her up and carry her straight to his bed.

But a bird calling overhead suddenly brought Jodi to her senses; white-faced and shaking, she pulled away from him. How on earth could she have allowed that to happen? Her mouth stung slightly and she had to resist the temptation to run her tongue-tip over it—to comfort it because it was missing the touch of Leo's? She ached from head to foot and she had started to tremble. Shocked to her heart by her lack of self-control, she cried out to him in a low tortured voice, 'Don't you ever touch me again…ever!'

And then she was gone, turning on her heel to flee in wretchedness, her heart throbbing with pain and self-contempt, refusing to stop as she heard Leo calling after her.

Jodi was still trembling when she reached the security of her own home. She had heard a rumour in the village that Ashton House had a tenant, but it had never occurred to her that it might be Leo Jefferson. Nigel had warned her that Leo had said that the negotiations over which of the factories he intended to close were likely to be protracted, but why did he have to move here to Frampton?

She felt as though there wasn't a single aspect of her life he hadn't now somehow penetrated and invaded.

Or a single aspect of herself?

Hurriedly she walked into her small kitchen and started to prepare her supper. Nigel had rung earlier and suggested they have dinner together, but Jodi had told him she was too busy, worried that if she saw him she might inadvertently betray the plans for the demonstration the following day.

Not that they were doing anything illegal, but she knew that Nigel would not entirely approve of her involvement in what was going to happen and would try his best to dissuade her.

She loved her cousin very much, they were in many ways as close as if they had been brother and sister, and she knew how shocked he would be if he was to learn how she had behaved with Leo Jefferson. She felt ashamed herself…but what was making her feel even worse were the dreadful dreams she kept having in which she relived what had happened—and enjoyed it.

Swallowing hard, Jodi tried to concentrate on what she was doing, but somehow she had lost her appetite. For food, that was. Standing in the garden earlier with Leo, there had been a moment when she had looked up at him, at his mouth, and she had never felt so hungry in her life…

Leo woke up with a start, wondering where he was at first, in the unfamiliarity of his new bedroom at Ashton House. He had been dreaming about Jodi and not for the first time. Reaching for the bedside lamp, he switched it on. The house had been repainted prior to being let and the smell of fresh paint still hung faintly on the air. Leo got out of bed and padded over to the window, pushing back the curtains to stare into the moonlit garden.

In his sleep he had remembered something about Jodi that disturbed him. Something he had not previously properly registered, but something that, knowing what he did now, made perfect sense!

Was it merely his imagination or had there really been a certain something about Jodi's body that might mean he had in fact been her first lover?

No, it was absurd that he should think any such thing. Totally absurd. She had been so uninhibited, so passionate…

But what if he was right? What if, in addition to having unwittingly drunk the alcoholic concoction supplied by her cousin and fallen asleep, she had been totally inexperienced?

Leo swallowed hard, aware of how very difficult he was finding it to use the word 'virgin', even in the privacy of his own thoughts.

But surely if that had been the case she would have said something.

Such as what? he derided himself. *Oh, by the way, before I went to bed with you I was a virgin.*

No, that would not be her style at all. She was far too independent, had far too much pride.

But if she had been a virgin…

At no point in the proceedings had she suggested that they should be thinking in terms of having safe sex, and he had certainly not been prepared either emotionally or practically to take on that responsibility, which meant…

There was no way Leo could sleep now. So far as

Jodi's sexual health was concerned, and his own, if he was right and she had been a virgin, he knew he need have no worries, but when it came to the risk of an unplanned pregnancy—that was a very different matter. And one surely that must be concerning Jodi herself.

He would very definitely have to talk to her now, and insist that she give him the answers to his questions.

Closing his eyes, he forced himself to recall every single second of the hours they had spent together—not that there was really any force involved, after all, his body and his senses had done precious little else other than relive the event ever since it had happened. But this time it was different, this time he was looking for clues, signs that he might have previously missed.

There had been that sweetly wonderful closeness between them in their most intimate moments, the feeling of her body being tightly wrapped around him. But she had said nothing. Given no indication that... What in hell's name had she been doing? he wondered, suddenly as angry for her as though she were his personal responsibility.

She was a schoolteacher, for heaven's sake. She was supposed to behave responsibly!

If she had been a virgin it put a completely different complexion on the whole situation. He was perhaps more Italian than he had ever previously realised, Leo recognised wryly as he felt an atavistic sense of male protectiveness engulf him, and with it an even more unexpected sense of pride. Because he had been her first lover? Because she might have accidentally conceived his child? Just how chauvinistic was he?

His mother, of course, would be overjoyed. A grandchild, and the kind of daughter-in-law she would wholly approve of and love showing off to her Italian relatives.

Whoa…Leo cautioned himself. These were very dangerous and foolish thoughts that had no business whatsoever clogging up his head.

For one insane moment he actually wondered if his mother might have gone ahead and got her village wise woman to put some kind of a love spell on him. Then reality resurfaced.

There was only one person to blame for the situation he was in and that one person was himself. He could, after all, have resisted Jodi. She was a woman, small and slender, weighing, he guessed, something around a hundred and twenty pounds, whilst he was a man, taller, heavier, and perfectly capable of having stopped her had he so wanted to.

Only he hadn't…

Have a heart, he protested to himself; she was there, warm, wanton, beddable, and totally and completely irresistible. It made him ache right through to the soles of his feet right now just to think about it.

Leo grimaced as he felt his body's unmistakable reaction to his thoughts.

He wanted her in a way that was totally alien to anything he had ever experienced before.

He wanted her. He wanted her. Oh, heavens, how he wanted her!

Jodi gave a tiny moan in her sleep, her lips forming Leo's name, and then abruptly she was awake, the reality of her situation blotting out the delicious pleasure of her lost dream.

She had felt so much safer when Leo Jefferson had not known who she was, when he had for some incomprehensible reason believed she was in cahoots with Jeremy Driscoll. Jeremy Driscoll! Jodi gave a brief shudder. Loathsome man!

One of the women who was going to be demonstrating had said at their committee meeting that she had seen Jeremy at the factory, coming out of a disused storeroom. He hadn't seen her and she had said that he had been behaving very furtively.

None of the workers liked Jeremy, and Jodi had wondered just exactly what he had been doing at the factory when it now belonged to Leo. Not that it was any concern of hers. No, her concern was much closer to home.

She had come so close to betraying herself this evening when Leo had been questioning her. The last thing she wanted was for him to realise that, far from being the experienced sensualist he obviously thought she was, she had, in fact, been a virgin before she had taken it into her idiotic head to go to bed with him.

And the reason she didn't want him to know the truth was because she was terrified that if he did he might start questioning just why she had been so compulsively attracted to him, so totally unable to resist the temptation he had represented.

She could, of course, always claim that, as a woman in her twenties, she had begun to see her virginity as a burden she wanted to free herself from, but somehow she doubted that he would believe her. He was too shrewd, too perceptive for that.

If he should ever find out just how she had felt about him when she had seen him in the hotel foyer Jodi knew that she would just die of embarrassment and humiliation.

But of course it was totally impossible that he should find out, wasn't it? Because only she knew.

And only she was going to know.

And only she knew that until she had met him she had been a virgin, and this evening she had as good as told him. That had been a mistake, yes, she allowed judiciously, but it was a mistake she had learned from. A mistake she most certainly was not going to be repeating.

She pulled the covers up more closely around herself. In the dream she had just woken from Leo had been wrapping her in his arms whilst he tenderly stroked her skin and even more tenderly kissed her lips…

What on earth was she? A born-again teenager indulging in a fantasy? She was not going to dream about him again, she told herself sternly. She was not!

The first Leo knew about the demonstration was when he received a phone call from a local radio station asking if he would like to comment on the situation.

Several other calls later he had elicited the information that the demonstration was non-violent, protesting against the factory being closed down.

Meetings he had already arranged with a large haulage group who were interested in potentially acquiring the site of the motorway-based factory meant that Leo was unable to go to Frampton himself until later on in the day, but he did speak with the leader of the group to set up a meeting with them to discuss the situation.

Although he was not prepared to say so at this stage,

Leo had virtually made up his mind that he would keep the Frampton factory open. This decision had nothing whatsoever to do with Jodi Marsh, of course.

Later in the day, when the police rang him to inform him that they intended to monitor the situation at the demonstration, Leo told them that he had every confidence that things would be resolved peacefully.

It was four o'clock, and there was no way he could leave London until at least five. His mind started to wander. What was Jodi doing now? He really did need to talk to her; if there was the remotest chance that she might have conceived his child then he needed to know about it.

Jodi glanced a little anxiously over her shoulder. She had joined the demo an hour ago, straight from school. At first things had been quiet and peaceful, and the leader had told her that Leo Jefferson had been in touch with him to organise a meeting for the following day. But then to everyone's surprise, half an hour ago Jeremy Driscoll had arrived. At first he had demanded that they open the factory gates to allow him access and when they had refused Jeremy had got out of the car. A small scuffle had ensued, but ultimately Jeremy had been allowed to walk into the office block.

He was still inside it, but ten minutes ago a police car had drawn up several yards away from the demonstrators, quickly followed by a reporter and a photographer from the local paper.

Now the original peaceful mood of the picketers had changed to one of hostile aggression as Jeremy emerged from the building, and one of the demonstrators to whom

Jeremy had been particularly verbally abusive on his way into the factory caught sight of him.

'You don't really think that this is going to make any difference to Jefferson's decision to close this place down, do you?' Jodi could hear Driscoll challenging her fellow demonstrator contemptuously.

'He's agreed to meet with us in the morning,' the other man was retaliating.

'And you think that means he's going to listen to what you have to say! More fool you. He's already decided that this place isn't viable and who can blame him, with a lazy, good-for-nothing workforce like you lot? It's because of you that we've had to sell the place. Everyone knows that...'

Jodi gave a small indignant gasp as she heard him.

'That's not true,' she interjected firmly, causing Jeremy to turn to look at her.

'My God, you!' he breathed. 'I suppose I should have guessed,' he sneered as he gave Jodi's jeans and T-shirt-clad body a deliberately lascivious stare. 'This isn't going to do you any favours with the school board, is it? But then, of course, your precious school will end up being closed down along with the factory, won't it? Looks as if I shall be getting my building land after all.' He smirked as he started to walk purposefully towards Jodi. People tried to stop him, but he was too quick for them.

As he moved towards Jodi one of the men started to step protectively between them. He was only a young man, nowhere near as heavily built as Jeremy, and Jodi winced as she saw the force with which Jeremy thrust him to one side.

The young man retaliated, and suddenly it seemed to Jodi as though all hell had broken loose; people were shouting, shoving, the police car doors were opening, and then before she could move, to her shock, Jeremy had suddenly taken hold of her and was dragging her across the factory forecourt.

Instinctively she tried to resist him, hitting out at him as he deliberately manhandled her; her panic was that of any woman fearing a man she knew to be her enemy, and had nothing whatsoever to do with her role in the demonstration. Jeremy dragged her towards one of the advancing police officers, claiming to them that she had deliberately assaulted him.

'I insist that you arrest her, officer,' Jodi could hear him saying as he gave her a nastily victorious look. 'I shall probably press charges for assault.'

Jodi tried to protest her innocence, but she was already being bundled towards the police van that had screamed to a halt alongside the car.

Jodi blinked in the light from the flashbulb as the hovering photographer took their picture.

The police station was busy. Jodi couldn't believe what was happening to her. A stern-looking sergeant she didn't recognise was beginning to charge them all. Jodi was feeling sick. Her head ached; she felt grubby and frightened. There was a bruise on her arm where Jeremy Driscoll had manhandled her.

'Name...'

Jodi flinched as she realised that the sergeant was speaking to her.

'Er—Jodi Marsh,' she began. Supporting the workforce by taking part in a peaceful demonstration was one thing. Ending up being charged and possibly thrown into a police cell was quite definitely another. She couldn't bear to think about what the more conservative parents of her pupils were going to say, never mind the school governors or the education authority.

'Excuse me, Officer.'

She was quite definitely going to faint, Jodi decided as she heard the unmistakable sound of Leo Jefferson's voice coming from immediately behind her.

Something about Leo's calm manner captured the sergeant's attention. Putting down his pen, he looked at him.

Leo had arrived at the factory gates just in time to hear from those who were still there what had happened.

'Yes, and they even took the schoolteacher away,' one of the onlookers had informed Leo with relish, wondering why on earth his comment should have caused his listener to turn round and head straight back to his car with such a grim look on his face.

'I'm Leo Jefferson,' Leo introduced himself to the sergeant. 'I own the factory.'

'You own it.' The sergeant was frowning now. 'According to our records, it was a Mr Jeremy Driscoll who reported that there was a problem.'

'Maybe he did, but I am quite definitely the owner of the factory,' Leo reiterated firmly. 'Can you tell me exactly what's happened, Officer. Only, as I understand it, the demonstrators were peaceful and I had in fact arranged to meet with them in the morning.'

'Well, that's as maybe, sir, but we were telephoned

from the factory by Mr Driscoll who said that he was not being allowed to leave and that both he and the property had been threatened with violence. Once we got there a bit of a scuffle broke out and this young lady here...' he indicated Jodi '...actually attempted to assault Mr Driscoll.'

Jodi could feel her face crimsoning with mortification as she leapt immediately to her own defence, denying it. 'I did no such thing. He was the one who attacked me...' To her horror, she could actually feel her eyes filling with childish tears.

'I think there must have been a mistake,' Leo Jefferson was saying. Although she couldn't bring herself to turn round and look at him, Jodi could feel him moving closer to her, and for some insane reason she felt that instinctively her body sought the warmth and protection of his.

'I happen to know Miss Marsh very well indeed. In fact she was at the factory on my behalf, as my representative,' Leo lied coolly. 'I cannot imagine for a second that she would have assaulted Mr Driscoll.'

The sergeant was frowning.

'Well, my officers have informed me that he was most insistent she be arrested,' he told Leo. 'He said that he intended to press charges against her for assault.'

Jodi gave a small, stifled sob.

'Indeed. Well, in that case I shall have to press charges against him for trespass,' Leo informed the sergeant. 'He quite definitely did not have my permission to enter the factory, and I rather imagine that the revenue authorities will be very interested to know what he was doing there. There are some account books missing that they are very anxious to see.'

Jodi gave a small start as she listened to him, impulsively turning round to tell Leo quickly, 'The mother of one of my pupils mentioned that she saw him coming out of one of the unused storerooms.' Her voice started to fade away as she saw the way Leo was looking at her arm.

'Is Driscoll responsible for that?' he demanded dangerously.

Without waiting for her to reply he turned to the desk sergeant and said with determined authority, 'I understand that you may have to charge Miss Marsh, but in the meantime, Officer, I wonder if you would be prepared to release her into my care. I promise that I won't let her out of my sight.'

The desk sergeant studied them both. He had a full custody suite and no spare cells, and he could see no real reason why Jodi shouldn't be allowed to leave if Leo Jefferson was prepared to vouch for her.

'Very well,' he acknowledged. 'But you will have to take full responsibility for her, and for ensuring that she returns here in the morning to be formally charged if Mr Driscoll insists on going ahead.'

'You have my word on it,' Leo responded promptly, and then before Jodi could say anything he had turned her round and was gently ushering her out into the summer night.

To her own chagrin, Jodi discovered that she was actually crying.

'It's the shock,' she heard Leo saying to her as he

guided her towards his car. 'Don't worry, you'll be OK once we get you home.'

'I want a bath…and some clean clothes,' Jodi told him in a voice she barely recognised as her own.

'The bath I can provide; the clothes we shall have to collect from your house on the way to mine,' Leo replied promptly.

'Yours!' Jodi's forehead creased as she allowed Leo to fasten the passenger seat belt around her. 'But I want to go to my own home.'

'You can't, I'm afraid,' Leo told her. 'The sergeant released you into my care, remember, and I have to produce you at the station in the morning.'

'But I can't stay with you,' Jodi protested.

'I'm sorry, Jodi.' Leo's voice was unexpectedly kind. 'You have to.'

'I didn't really assault Jeremy.' Jodi tried to defend herself. 'He was the one…' She stopped and bit her lip, her stomach clenching on a leap of nervous shock as she saw the ferocity in Leo's eyes as he turned to study her.

'If he hurt you… Did he, Jodi?'

When she looked away from him Leo cursed himself for the intensity of his own reaction. He had quite plainly shocked and frightened her, and she had already been frightened more than enough for one night.

'I thought the demonstration was supposed to be a peaceful one,' he commented as he drove back towards the village.

'It was,' Jodi acknowledged. 'But Jeremy was very confrontational and somehow things got out of hand. Is it true that he's being investigated?'

'Yes,' Leo told her briefly, 'but I shouldn't really have said so, I don't suppose.'

When they reached her cottage he insisted on going inside with her and waiting until she had packed a small case of necessities, and Jodi felt too disorientated to be able to have the strength to resist.

Jeremy Driscoll's manner towards her had left her feeling vulnerable, and she couldn't help remembering how when she had won her battle with him to retain the playing field for the school he had threatened to get even with her. He was a vengeful and dangerous man, and for tonight at least, loath though she was to admit it, she knew she would feel far safer sleeping under Leo Jefferson's roof than under her own.

CHAPTER SIX

'WHEN was the last time you had something to eat?'

Leo's prosaic question as he unlocked his front door and ushered Jodi into the hallway of the house made her give him an uncertain look.

She had been steeling herself for, if not his hostility, then certainly some sharply incisive questions. The fact that he seemed more worried about her personal welfare than anything else was thoroughly disconcerting—but nowhere near as disconcerting as the relief and sense of security it had given her to have him take charge in the way that he had done.

'Lunchtime.' She answered his question on autopilot, whilst most of her attention was given to what she was feeling at a much deeper level. 'But I'm not hungry.'

'That's because you're still in shock,' Leo told her gently. 'The kitchen is this way.'

At any other time Jodi knew that she would have been fascinated to see the inside of the house she had admired so much, but right now she felt as though her ability to take in anything was overwhelmed by the events of the evening.

As Leo had suggested, she suspected that she was suffering from shock. Otherwise, why would she be so apathetically allowing Leo to make all her decisions for her? She let him guide her firmly to a kitchen chair and urge her into it, whilst he busied himself opening cupboards and then the fridge door, insisting that the light supper he was going to make them both would help her to sleep.

'Which reminds me,' he added several minutes later as he served her with an impressively light plate of scrambled eggs, 'I'm afraid that you will have to sleep in my bedroom, since it's the only one that's properly furnished at the moment; I can sleep downstairs on a sofa.'

'No,' Jodi protested immediately, praying that he wouldn't guess the reason for the hot colour suddenly burning her face. The very thought of sleeping in his bed was bringing back memories she had no wish to have surfacing at any time, but most especially when the man responsible for them was seated opposite her.

To her consternation, Leo shook his head at her instinctive refusal, telling her calmly, 'It's all right, I can guess what you must be thinking, but you don't need to worry.'

Jodi tensed. How could he possibly know what she was thinking? And if he really did then how dared he treat it and her as though...?

As she tried to gather her thoughts into a logical enough order to challenge him she heard him continuing, 'The cleaning team came today, and they will have changed the bed linen.'

Jodi almost choked on her scrambled eggs as relief flooded through her. He hadn't realised what she was thinking after all; hadn't realised just what piercingly sensual and shocking images the mention of his bed had aroused for her.

But at least his comments had given her time to gain

some control of her thoughts, and for her to remember that she was supposed to be a sensible, mature adult.

'I can't possibly take your bed,' she informed Leo in what she hoped was a cool and businesslike voice.

'Why not?' Leo demanded, giving her a quizzical look, and then threw her into complete turmoil as he reminded her softly, 'After all, it isn't as though you haven't done so before.'

As the blood left her face and then rushed back to it in a wave of bright pink Jodi felt her hand trembling so much that she had to grip the mug of tea Leo had given her with both hands to prevent herself from spilling its contents.

She knew that she was overreacting, but somehow she just couldn't stop herself.

Leo's teasing comment had not just embarrassed her, it had left her feeling humiliated as well, Jodi recognised as she felt the unwanted prick of her tears threatening to expose her vulnerability to him.

But even as she struggled fiercely to blink them away, Leo was already apologising.

'I'm sorry,' he offered. 'I shouldn't have said that.' Leo paused, watching her, mentally berating himself for offending her. It amazed him how much discovering that he had been wrong in his earlier assessment of the situation had changed what he felt about her.

The last thing he wanted to do was to hurt her in any way, but there were still certain issues they needed to address—together—and, although he had not deliberately tried to lead up to them, now that the subject had been introduced perhaps he should seize the opportunity to discuss his concerns with her.

'I know that this perhaps isn't the best time in the world to say this,' he began quietly, 'but we really do need to talk, Jodi...'

Unsteadily Jodi put her mug down on the table.

'Is that why you brought me here?' she demanded as fiercely as she could. 'So that you could cross-examine me? If you think for one minute that just because you saved me from a night in prison I am going to repay you by betraying the others involved in the demonstration, I'm afraid you'd better take me back to the station right now—'

'Jodi.' Leo interrupted her passionate tirade as gently as he could. 'I don't want to talk to you about the problems at the factory, or the demonstration.'

As he watched her eyes shadow with suspicion Leo wondered what she would say if he was to tell her that right now there was only one person and one problem on his mind, and that was her!

'I've already arranged a meeting with representatives of the factory workforce for tomorrow, when I intend to discuss my proposals for the future of the factory with them,' he told her calmly.

'Yes, I heard.' Jodi suddenly felt totally exhausted, drained to the point where simply to think was a superhuman effort. 'Then what did you want to talk to me about?' she asked him warily.

Leo could see how tired she looked and he berated himself for his selfishness. She was still in shock. She needed to rest and recuperate, not be plagued by questions.

'It doesn't matter,' he told her gently. 'Look, why

don't you go to bed? You look completely done in...'
Leo reached out to help her out of the chair.

Sensing that he was about to touch her, Jodi felt her
defences leap into action, knowing all too well just how
vulnerable she was likely to be to any kind of physical
contact with him right now. She sprang up out of the
chair, almost stumbling in her haste to avoid contact with
him, and in doing so precipitated the very thing she had
been so desperate to prevent. As Leo reached out to
steady her his hands grasped her arms. As he took the
weight of her fall against his body he closed the distance
between them.

It was just a week since she had first seen him, a
handful of days, that was all, so how on earth could it
be that she was reacting to him as though she was starving for physical contact as though the sudden feel of him
against her answered a craving that nothing else could
hope to appease?

It was as if just the act of leaning against him fulfilled
and completed her, made her feel whole again, made her
feel both incredibly strong and helplessly weak. She felt
that she had found the purpose in life for which she had
been created and yet at the same time she hated herself
for her neediness.

Mutely she pushed against his chest, demanding her
release. Leo obeyed the demand of her body language,
asking her gruffly, 'Are you OK?'

'Yes, I'm fine,' Jodi responded as she stepped back
from him and turned away, ducking into the shadows so
that he couldn't see the aching hunger in her expression.

How had things possibly come to this? How had she

come to this? Where had her feelings come from? They were totally alien in their intensity and their ferocity.

Leo held the kitchen door open for her. Shakily she walked out into the hallway.

Leo accompanied her to the bottom of the stairs. Jodi began to climb them, her heart bumping heavily against the wall of her chest. She dared not look at Leo, dared not do anything that might betray to him how she was feeling.

'It's the second door on the left along the landing,' she could hear him telling her. 'You'll find clean towels and everything in the bathroom. I'll go and get your bag for you and leave it outside the bedroom door.'

He was telling her as plainly as though he had used the words themselves that she need not fear a repetition of what had happened in his hotel bedroom, Jodi recognised. Which was surely very thoughtful and gentlemanly of him. So why wasn't she feeling more appreciative, more relieved? Why was she, to be blunt about it, actually feeling disappointed?

Wearily Jodi made her way to the top of the stairs.

As he stood watching the tiredness with which she moved Leo ached to be able to go after her, gather her up protectively in his arms. He deliberately forced himself to turn round and go out to the car to bring in Jodi's bag.

The look of confusion and despair he had seen on her face in the police station had prompted him into a course of action he now recognised as riven with potential hazards.

When he returned with Jodi's bag he took it upstairs, knocked briefly outside his closed bedroom door and went straight back downstairs again, shutting himself in the sitting room.

Jodi was standing staring out of the bedroom window when she heard Leo's knock. She deliberately made herself count to ten—very slowly—before going to open the door, and then told herself that she was relieved and not disappointed to find that the landing was empty and there was no sign of Leo.

Both the bedroom and the bathroom adjoining it were furnished so impersonally that they might almost have been hotel rooms; but thinking of hotel rooms in connection with Leo aroused thoughts and feelings for her that were far from impersonal. Jodi hastily tried to divert her thoughts to less dangerous channels as she went into the bathroom and prepared for bed.

Now that she was on her own she knew that she ought to be thinking about the morning and the possibility of having to face the charges that Jeremy Driscoll had threatened to bring against her—a daunting prospect indeed, but somehow nowhere near as daunting as having to acknowledge just how strong her feelings for Leo were.

That comment he had made to her earlier about her previous appropriation of his bed!

It had made her feel embarrassed and even humiliated, yes, but it had made her remember how wildly wonderful it had felt—she had felt—to be there in his arms. In his life? But she wasn't in his life, and he wasn't in hers, not really. All they had done was have sex together, and every woman—even a schoolteacher—knew that for men the act of sex could be enjoyed with less emotional involvement than they might feel consuming a bar of chocolate—nice at the time but quickly forgotten.

She crawled into Leo's bed—totally sober this time! The bed smelled of clean, fresh linen, as anonymous and bereft of any tangible sign of Leo as the room itself. Curling up in the centre of the large bed, she closed her eyes, but despite her exhaustion sleep evaded her.

She was almost too overtired to sleep, she recognised, the anxieties filling her thoughts, refusing to allow her to relax. She closed her eyes and started to breathe slowly and deeply.

Downstairs, Leo was finding sleep equally hard to come by. He had work to do that could have occupied his time and his thoughts, but instead he found that he was pacing the sitting-room floor, thinking about Jodi. Worrying about Jodi, and not just because he had now realised just what an awkward situation they could both be in because of their shared night together.

That bruise on her arm caused by Jeremy Driscoll had made him feel as though he could quite happily have torn the other man limb from limb and disposed of his carcass to the nearest hungry carnivore. The mere thought of him even touching Jodi...

Abruptly he stopped pacing. What the devil was happening to him? Did he really need to ask that? he mocked himself inwardly. He was in love. This was love. He was transformed into a man he could barely recognise. A man who behaved and thought illogically, a man driven by his emotions, a man who right now...

He froze as he heard a sound from upstairs, and then

strode towards the door, wrenching it open just in time to hear it again, a high-pitched sound of female misery.

Leo took the stairs two at a time, flinging open the bedroom door and striding across the floor to where Jodi lay in the middle of the bed.

She was awake; in the darkness he could see her eyes shining, but she was lying as silently still as though she dared not breathe, never mind move.

'Jodi, what is it?' he demanded.

A wash of shaky relief sluiced through Jodi as she heard and recognised Leo's voice. She had been dreaming about Jeremy Driscoll. A most awful dream, full of appalling and nameless nightmare terrors. It had been the sound of her own muffled scream of sheer panic that had woken her, and for a couple of heartbeats after Leo had thrown open the bedroom door she had actually believed that he was Jeremy.

Now, though, the sound of his voice had reassured her, banishing the nightmare completely.

Too relieved to think of anything else other than the fact that he had rescued her from the terror which had been pursuing her, she turned towards him, telling him, 'I was having the most horrid dream…about Jeremy Driscoll…'

Just saying his name was still enough to make her shudder violently as she struggled to sit up so that she could talk properly to Leo, who was now leaning over the bed towards her.

She could see the anxiety in his eyes now that her own had accustomed themselves to the night-time shadows of the room, their darkness softened by the summer moonlight outside.

'I'm sorry if I disturbed you.' She began to apologise and then checked as she saw that he was still fully dressed.

Was the sitting-room sofa so uncomfortable that he hadn't even bothered trying to sleep on it, or did the fact that he still had his clothes on have something to do with her presence here in his house? Was he afraid that she might try to seduce him a second time?

'What is it? What's wrong?'

The speed with which he had read her expression caught Jodi off guard. Her defences, already overloaded by the events of the day, gave up on her completely.

'You're still dressed,' she told him in a low voice. 'You haven't been to bed; if that's because—'

But before she could voice her fears Leo was interrupting her.

'It's because right now the only bed I want to be in is already occupied, and denied to me,' he told her huskily. 'Unless, of course, you're prepared to change your mind and share it with me?'

Leo knew that he was doing exactly what he had told himself he must not do under any kind of circumstances; that he was behaving like a predator, taking advantage of both Jodi's vulnerability and her current dependence on him, but he still couldn't stop himself. Just the sight of her sitting there in his bed, her slim bare arms wrapped around her hunched-up knees as she looked uncertainly up at him, was enough to make him know that he was prepared to be damned for this eternity and every eternity beyond it just to have her in his arms again, to be granted the opportunity to hold her, touch her, kiss her, caress her.

He wasn't still dressed because he didn't want her, Jodi realised, or because he was afraid that she might embarrass them both by coming on to him. She could feel her whole body starting to tremble beneath the on-rush of wild excitement that was roaring through her.

Leo groaned her name, unable to hold back his long-ing for her. He reached for her, wrapping her in his arms, his mouth so passionately urgent that the sound of her name was lost beneath his kiss.

Jodi knew that she should resist him, that she should insist that he release her, so why instead of doing so was she clinging shamelessly to him? She opened her mouth eagerly to the demanding probe of his tongue, her whole body racked with a raw, aching hunger for him.

She had almost begun to convince herself that their previous lovemaking couldn't possibly have been as good as she remembered, that she had exaggerated it, romanticised it, turning it in her mind into an implausible state of perfection that was total fantasy. Now, shock-ingly, she knew her memory *had* been at fault, although not in the way that she expected!

Leo's lovemaking had not been as wonderful as she had remembered—it had been even better! More plea-surable, more intoxicating…

As her body relived the pleasure his had given her Jodi knew that there was no point in trying to stop her-self from responding to him, no way she could stop her-self from wanting him.

She heard the small, tortured groan that filled her own throat as she feasted greedily on his kiss. The touch of his mouth against hers was like receiving a life-giving transfusion, she told herself dizzily as Leo cupped her face in his hands and held her a willing captive and kissed her with an intimacy that almost stopped her heart.

Jodi trembled and then shuddered as the pleasure of being so close to him filled her, running through her nervous system like pure adrenalin.

'We shouldn't be doing this.' Jodi could hear the total lack of conviction in the longing-filled softness of her voice.

'I know,' Leo responded rawly. 'But I just can't stop myself.'

'I don't want you to stop!'

Had she really said that? Jodi was shocked by her own wanton lack of restraint, and shocked too by the discovery that somehow or other she had already managed to unfasten half of the buttons of Leo's shirt.

Beneath her explorative fingertips she could feel the soft silkiness of his body hair.

She leaned forward, breathing in the scent of his skin with deliberate sensuality.

A rush of sensation flooded her, a dizzying kaleidoscope of emotions, recognition—she would recognise his scent anywhere—exaltation, just to have the freedom to be so intimate, so possessively womanly with him. Inhaling his scent only served to remind her of just how many other ached-for intimacies she could enjoy with him. She felt a surge of power, of female strength, knowing that she was responsible for the acceleration of his breathing.

Leo felt himself shudder from top to toe, totally unable to control the fierceness of his response to Jodi. It felt as if every sensation he had ever experienced had just been intensified a thousandfold. Even the simple act of breathing seemed to fill his whole body, his every sense with a heart-rocking awareness of her and longing for her.

This wasn't, he recognised, mere lust, this was the big one; *the* one. She, Jodi, was his one and only. But, he knew instinctively, he couldn't tell her so, not now, not yet; what they were building between them was still too fragile.

He groaned out loud again as Jodi kissed his bared torso. His desire for her ran like fire through his body, the sweetest form of torture.

Swiftly Leo removed the rest of his clothes, never once losing eye contact with Jodi whilst he did so.

He warned himself that she might see in his eyes his love for her, but he couldn't make himself break the contact between them that seemed to be binding them so intimately close together.

In her eyes he could see wonderment, uncertainty, longing, and even a little old-fashioned female shock. Her body clenched when he cupped the tender ball of her shoulder with one hand whilst tugging off the last of his clothes with the other, but she didn't make any attempt to break the gaze that was locking them together.

Somehow the silent visual bonding between them was as sensually charged as touching.

His body ached intolerably for her, and so too did his heart, his entire being.

'Jodi.' He whispered her name again as he gathered her closer, finally breaking their eye contact to look down at her mouth and then up into her eyes again before slowly brushing his mouth against hers.

Jodi felt as though she was going to explode with the sheer force of the sensual tension building up inside her.

It was a good job she was not some impressionable teenager, she told herself, otherwise she would be in danger of deceiving herself that the way Leo was looking at her, as though he wanted to communicate something deeply meaningful, meant that he really cared about her.

She knew that she ought to bring what was happening between them to an end now, before things went any further, but Leo was taking hold of her, brushing his mouth against hers once more in a way that aroused in her such a sweetly aching desire.

Beneath his mouth Leo could feel Jodi's parting; he could taste the sweet exhaled breath, feel the soft little tremor that ran through her body as she nestled closer to him.

Leo was stroking her skin with his hands, making her ache and quiver, his mouth leaving hers to caress the vulnerable place where her shoulder joined her throat, nuzzling little kisses up to her ear whilst his tongue-tip investigated its delicate whorls. Each small sensation coalesced, melded together until she was on fire with the heat of the need he was creating inside her.

Her breasts, swelling, peaking, ached for the touch of his hands. As though he seemed to know it he shaped them, stroking the pads of his thumbs over the erect crests of her nipples.

Jodi trembled and moaned, closed her eyes, welcoming the velvet darkness that lapped protectively around her, and then opened them again on a gasp of piercingly sweet pleasure as she felt Leo's mouth against first one breast and then the other.

Her fingers dug into the hard muscles of his back, her body arching in an irresistible mixture of supplication and temptation.

Leo was kissing her belly, rimming her navel with his tongue. Her fingers clenched in his thick, dark hair. Her intention had been to push him away, but helplessly her hands stilled as he moved lower and then lower still.

Such intimacy was surely only for the most beloved of lovers, but Jodi couldn't find the strength to resist or deny what he was giving her; her body, like her emotions, clenched first against what was happening, and then gave in.

As he moved his body over hers and entered her Leo immediately felt the first fierce contraction of her release. His own body leapt to meet and complete it, his emotions as well as his senses taking hotly satisfying pleasure in knowing they were sharing this moment together.

Jodi cried out Leo's name, wrapping herself around him, holding him deep inside her, where she had so much wanted him to be. It felt so wondrously right to have him there, a part of her, now and for always.

'Leo.'

She sighed his name in exhausted pleasure as tears of fulfilment washed her eyes and flowed onto her face, to be tenderly licked away by Leo, before he reached out to wrap her in his arms.

She was asleep before they closed fully around her.

CHAPTER SEVEN

LEO allowed himself a small smile of satisfaction when he finally replaced the telephone receiver at the end of what had been a long half-hour of diplomatic discussion with the police.

He had earlier spent a very terse and determined five minutes on the telephone to Jeremy, informing him of the fact that he would most certainly be placing charges against *him* for unlawfully being on the company's premises if he was to go ahead and try to accuse Jodi of anything. Did he, Jeremy, Leo had asked grimly, possess the same physical evidence of this supposed assault that Jodi did of his unwarranted manhandling of her? Jeremy had blustered and tried to counter-threaten, but in the end he had given way.

The police had been rather less easy to negotiate with; for a start, as the superintendent had told Leo coolly, they did not take too kindly to the demands the demonstration at the factory had placed on their very limited financial budget, and they were certainly not about to give out a message to the public that acts of violence were something they were prepared to permit.

Leo had protested that the demonstration had been intended to be a peaceful one, citing the fact that he, as the owner of the factory, did not feel it necessary to make any kind of complaint against his workforce, so then surely the matter could be allowed to rest. As it transpired, Leo discovered that in the end none of the protesters had actually been held overnight at the police station, and that Jodi would have been the only one of them who might have faced the prospect of charges, and that only because of the assault incident claimed by Jeremy.

Ultimately the police had agreed, that since Jeremy was prepared to drop his accusation, there was no real case against her and she did not need to return to the station.

He had, Leo recognised, barely an hour left to go before he was due to talk with the factory's workforce, and there was still that vitally important and delicate issue he needed to discuss with Jodi!

Showered and dressed, Jodi hesitated at the top of staircase. Although she had pretended to be asleep, she had been fully aware of Leo getting out of bed and leaving her.

How was it possible for a supposedly intelligent woman to make the same mistake twice?

As anxious as she was about what might lie ahead of her when she returned to the police station, she was even more concerned about her feelings for Leo. Her feelings? When was she going to have the courage to give them their proper name?

Her love!

A tiny sound somewhere between a denial and a moan bubbled in her throat. If only last night hadn't been so…so perfect. So everything she had ever wanted the intimacy she shared with the man she loved to be. If only Leo had been different, if only he had done something, anything, that had made her want to distance herself from him.

As she started to make her way down the stairs Leo suddenly appeared in the hallway, standing watching her, making her feel breathless and shaky, weak with the sheer power of her love for him.

'I've just finished speaking with the police,' Leo began.

'Yes, I haven't forgotten that I've got to go back,' Jodi informed him quickly. Somehow she managed to force herself to give him a tight proud look, which she hoped would tell him that she was completely unfazed by the prospect. 'I'm not sure just what the formalities will be.' Her voice startled to wobble slightly, despite her efforts to control it. 'Presumably I shall have to contact a lawyer.'

'There wouldn't be any point in you doing that,' Leo began to inform her, and then stopped as he saw the look of white-faced anxiety she was trying so valiantly to conceal from him. 'Jodi. It's all right,' he told her urgently. 'I—that is, the police have decided that there's no need for you to go back.'

Leo wasn't entirely sure why he had decided not to tell Jodi of the role he had played in that decision; it just seemed like the right choice to make.

'I don't have to go back?'

It wasn't just her voice that was trembling now, Leo recognised as he watched the relief shake her body. The urge to go to her and wrap her in his arms whilst he told her that he would never allow anything to hurt or frighten her ever again was so powerful that he had taken several steps towards her before he managed to pull himself back.

Jodi was convinced she must have misunderstood what Leo was telling her.

'You mean I don't have to go right now, today?' she questioned him uncertainly.

'I mean you don't have to go back ever,' Leo corrected her. Adding in a softly liquid voice, 'It's over, Jodi. There isn't anything for you to worry about.'

'But what about Jeremy Driscoll?' Jodi protested.

'Apparently he's changed his mind,' Leo told her carelessly, turning away from her as he did so.

There was no way he wanted Jodi to feel that she was under any kind of obligation to him for speaking to Jeremy.

He was still aware that last night he had to some extent coerced her into making love with him, at least emotionally. And when the time came for him to tell her how he felt about her he didn't want her to feel pressured in any way at all.

He had a right, he believed, to explain how he felt now and how his own fight against his feelings had led, in part, to his original misjudgement of her. But he was not going to use any kind of emotional blackmail to compel Jodi into saying she felt the same.

When it came to whether or not they had created a new life together; well, that was a very different matter. Leo would use any means possible to make sure he would be a presence in that child's life.

'Look, Jodi, I have to go out shortly,' he told her. 'But before I do, there's something we have to discuss.'

Jodi felt her stomach lurch, a cold feeling of dread swilling through her veins.

She knew what was coming, of course; what he was going to say to her…

'Last night was a mistake. I'm sorry. But I hope you understand…'

Mentally she steeled herself for the blow she knew was about to fall.

'Let's go into the kitchen,' Leo began unexpectedly. 'I've made some coffee, and you must be hungry.'

Hungry!

'I thought you were in a rush to go out,' Jodi tried to protest as Leo ushered her towards the kitchen.

'I've got an appointment I have to keep,' Leo agreed, 'but I can talk whilst you eat.'

Eat! Jodi knew there was no way she could do that, but still she allowed Leo to fill her a bowl of cereal, and pour them both a mug of coffee before he began quietly, 'The first time we met I made a grave misjudgement, not just of the situation, Jodi, but of you as well.'

Leo paused, as though he was searching for the right words, and Jodi began to stiffen defensively.

'I'm concerned, Jodi, that because of the…the circumstances surrounding the intimacy we've shared we may both be guilty of having neglected to—er—think through the consequences of our actions and do something to ensure…' Leo stopped and shook his head.

'Look, what I'm trying to say, Jodi, is that if there's any chance that you might be pregnant…well, then something will have to be arranged. I wouldn't want you to…'

Pregnant. Jodi's heart bumped and thudded against

her ribcage as she stared at Leo in mute shock. *'Something will have to be arranged...'* She tried to absorb the meaning of his words. Did he think for one minute that if she was carrying his child she would allow that precious new life to be 'arranged' away? She would never agree to anything like that. Never!

Her blood ran cold. She had been expecting him to tell her that last night had been a mistake, an impulse he now regretted, a mere sexual encounter which she wasn't to take seriously nor read anything meaningful into. But to know that he had already thought as far ahead as wanting to dispose of any possible consequences of their intimacy hurt her more than she felt able to cope with and, at the same time, made her more angry than anything else he had either said or done.

What was it he was really worried about? Fathering a child he didn't want, or having her make any kind of financial or emotional claims on him on behalf of that child? What sort of a woman did he think she was?

Before she could even think about what she was saying she told him quickly and sharply, 'There is no chance of me being...of anything like that.'

Her heart was still thumping as she spoke, but her reactions were instinctive and immediate. How could she possibly continue to love him after this?

Jodi sounded so coldly positive that Leo started to frown. Had he been wrong to presume that just because she wasn't experienced that meant that she was unprotected from the risk of pregnancy?

Before he could stop himself Leo heard himself insisting fiercely, 'But that night in my suite was your first time, and——'

'How could you possibly know that?' she demanded, oblivious in her anger of the fact that she herself had just confirmed his gut feelings. Without waiting for him to answer her she continued emotionally, 'Well, just because I happened to be…because you were my first…' she amended hurriedly, 'that does not mean that I am going to get pregnant!'

As she spoke Jodi was getting up from the table and storming out of the kitchen, telling Leo acidly as she did so, 'I'm going to get my things and then I'm going home right now. And I never want to see you again! From the moment you arrived in Frampton you've caused misery and made life impossible for everyone. And just let me tell you that there's absolutely no way I would ever want to inflict on my child the burden of having you for a father.'

'Are you sure you'll be all right?'

Jodi glowered at Leo as he reached out to open the passenger door of his car. It had been galling in the extreme after her outburst to be forced to accept his offer of a lift home.

'Well, I shall certainly be far better here in my own home than I was last night in yours, won't I?' she demanded with pointed iciness as Leo insisted on carrying her bag to her front door for her and waiting to see her safely inside.

As she gave in to the unwanted temptation to watch him drive away Jodi felt sick with fear for her future, and anger against herself.

She was surely too adult, too mature for this kind of emotional folly!

*   *   *

As he drove away from Jodi's cottage Leo discovered that he was actually grinding his teeth. The last thing he felt like doing right now was sitting down at the negotiating table. The only thing he wanted to do was to take hold of Jodi Marsh and tell her in no uncertain terms just how he felt about her, and what his life was going to be without her...

So much for his earlier high-minded promise to himself not to use any kind of emotional blackmail to press his suit, Leo reflected grimly. But those comments Jodi had made about not wanting him as a father for her child had hurt—and badly—and he had been within a breath of telling her in no uncertain terms that if her body was allowed to speak for itself it might have a very different story to tell. 'Because make no mistake about it, Jodi Marsh, your body damned well wanted me!'

To Leo's consternation he suddenly realised as the sound of his own voice filled the car that he was talking to himself! No wonder they called love a form of madness!

More drained by everything that had happened than she wanted to admit, Jodi suddenly discovered that she was craving the escape of sleep. She normally had buckets of energy, but these last couple of days she had felt physically drained. On her return home she went upstairs, intending to collect some washing, and then she saw her bed, and one thing led to another and...

It was the sound of her doorbell ringing that finally woke her. Realising that she had fallen deeply asleep, still fully dressed, she made her way groggily downstairs, her heart leaping frantically as she wondered if her visitor was Leo.

It had hurt her so badly this morning, after the wonderful night they had spent together, to know how desperate he was to distance himself from her and to make sure she knew that he didn't want her.

However, her visitor wasn't Leo, but Nigel her cousin. As she let him in he was waving a newspaper in front of her.

'You're on the front page,' he told her. 'Have you seen the paper yet?'

The front page! Jodi took the newspaper from him and studied it, her face burning with consternation and embarrassment as she studied the photograph of the previous evening's arrests.

'I was half expecting I was going to have to bail my strait-laced cousin out of prison,' Nigel joked as he made his way towards her small kitchen.

'Only, as I understand it, Leo got there before me.'

He shot Jodi a wry look as she demanded, 'Who told you that?'

'I rang the police station,' Nigel informed her. 'Reading between the lines, it sounds as if Leo must have put one hell of a lot of pressure on Jeremy Driscoll to get him to back off from charging you.'

To back off? Jodi began to frown.

'But Leo said that Jeremy had changed his mind,' she protested shakily.

'Yeah, but probably only after Leo had told him that if he didn't he would change it for him, if my guess is correct,' Nigel agreed derisively. 'Apparently Leo was on the phone to the police for nearly half an hour this morning, insisting that he did not want charges pressed against you, or any of the workforce. It seems to me that Leo must think an awful lot of you, little cousin, to go to so much trouble on your behalf,' Nigel teased her. 'This wouldn't be the beginning of a classic tale of romance between two adversaries, would it?' He grinned, his smile fading when he saw the look of white-faced despair Jodi was giving him. 'Are you OK?' he asked in concern.

'I'm fine,' Jodi lied.

'Feel like going out for a meal tonight?' Nigel suggested.

Jodi shook her head. 'No; I've got some work I need to prepare for school on Monday,' she told him, 'but thanks for asking.'

Nigel was almost at the front door, when he turned round and told her, 'Leo was meeting with the representatives of the factory this morning. Did he drop any hints about what he was going to say to them?'

'No, why should he?' she asked Nigel primly.

He was, she could see, giving her a worried look.

'Something's wrong; you're not your normal self, Jodi. What—?'

'Nothing's wrong,' she lied grittily. 'I'm just tired, that's all.'

She felt guilty about lying to Nigel, who was practically her best friend as well as her cousin, but what alternative did she really have?

A small, uncomfortable silence followed her denial, before Nigel turned to open the front door.

Jodi watched him go. She had been unfairly sharp with him, she knew, and ultimately she would have to apologise and explain, but not right now. Right now she just wasn't capable of doing anything so rational! All she really wanted to do was to think about Leo, and what Nigel had told her.

It had confused her to learn that Leo had intervened with the authorities on her behalf. After all, he had allowed her to believe that they had been the ones to contact him, and not, as Nigel had implied, the other way around.

It galled Jodi to know that she was in his debt—not that that made a single scrap of difference to what she felt about what he had said to her earlier. No way! Those words were words she would never forgive him for uttering. Still, she knew she would have to thank him for what he had done, and the sooner she got that onerous task over with the better! Gritting her teeth, she went upstairs to shower and get changed.

Leo saw Jodi as she walked up the drive towards the front door of Ashton House. He was standing in the room he was using as an office, having just completed a telephone call with his new partner in the haulage and distribution business he intended to site at the motorway-based factory.

As he had informed the representatives of the Frampton workforce earlier, he had now decided to keep that factory open, but it would be up to them to prove to him that he had made the right decision, with an increased output to ensure his business kept its competitive edge over its overseas rivals.

Despite the fact that it was a hot summer's day, Jodi

was wearing a very formal-looking black trouser suit, its jacket open over a white T-shirt.

Leo, in contrast, had changed into a pair of casual chinos on his return from his meeting, but that did not prevent Jodi from thinking how formidable he looked as he opened the door just as she reached out to ring the bell.

Formidably male, that was, she admitted to herself as he invited her into the house.

Why, oh, why did she have to feel this way about him? Her pain at loving him was laced with her furious anger at his unbelievably callous words of the morning.

Perhaps to him, a high-powered businessman, an unplanned child was just a problem to be disposed of, but there was no way she could contemplate taking such an unemotional course.

If she thought for one moment that there was the slightest chance that she could be pregnant... After all, she had lied to Leo when she had intimated that she had taken precautions to ensure that she did not conceive.

Now she was deliberately trying to frighten herself, Jodi decided firmly, dismissing her uncomfortable anxiety. She was not pregnant. Totally, definitely not.

And, besides, didn't she have enough to worry about?

As she followed Leo inside the house she began with determination, 'Nigel's been to see me. He says that I have you to thank for the fact that I did not have to return to the police station this morning.'

The way she delivered the words, with an extremely militant look in her eyes, made Leo curse her cousin silently.

'Jodi—' he began, but she shook her head, refusing to let him continue.

'Is it true?' she demanded.

'The police agreed with me that there was no reason to take things any further with any of those concerned in what essentially had been a peaceful demonstration,' Leo palliated.

'So it is true,' Jodi announced baldly. 'Why did you do it?' she asked him bitterly.

'So that you could have me under some kind of obligation to you? Why would you want that, or can I guess?' she demanded sarcastically. 'So that you could demand that I—?'

'Stop right there.'

Now it was Jodi's turn to fall silent as Leo glared furiously at her. Did she really think that he would stoop so low as to try to demand that she make love with him?

Beneath his anger, running much, much deeper, Leo could feel the savage, ripping claws of pain.

Jodi told herself that she wasn't going to back down or allow him to make her feel she was in the wrong. After what he had said this morning it seemed perfectly logical to her that he would consider using the fact that he had negotiated her freedom to demand that she acquiesce to his demands over an accidental pregnancy.

All the anguish she was feeling welled up inside her. Ignoring the oxygen-destroying tension crackling between them, and the anger she could see glinting in Leo's eyes, Jodi protested, 'You just don't care, do you? Feelings, human life—they don't matter to you. You're quite happy to close down the factory and put people out of work...'

And quite happy, too, to deny his child the right to live, Jodi reflected inwardly, the pain of that knowledge twisting her insides like acid—not just for the child she was positive she had not conceived but also for the destruction of her own foolish dreams.

Somewhere deep down inside herself she had seen him as a hero, a truly special man, imbued with all the virtues that women universally loved, especially the instinct to protect those weaker and more vulnerable than himself. It hurt to know just how wrong she had been.

Leo had had enough. How dared she accuse him of not having feelings? If he was as callous, as uncaring as she was accusing him of being, right now she would be lying under him on his bed whilst he...

As Leo fought to control the surging shock of his fierce desire he couldn't stop himself from retaliating savagely, 'If this is your way of trying to persuade me to keep the factory open, let me tell you the tactics you employed in my hotel suite would be far more effective.'

Leo knew the moment the words were out of his mouth that they were a mistake, but it was too late to recall them.

Jodi was looking at him with an expression of contemptuous loathing in her eyes, whilst her mouth...!

Leo had to swallow—hard—as he saw that small, betraying tremble of her firmly compressed lips. The same lips he had not such a very long time ago teased open with his tongue before...

Was that actually a groan Leo had just uttered? Jodi wondered with furious female anger. Well, he certainly deserved to be in pain after what he had just said to her!

It was only the sheer force of her anger that was keeping her from bursting into either incoherent speech or helpless emotional tears.

How could he have stooped so low as to throw that at her?

Well, he would quickly learn that she could be equally offensive!

'If I thought that such tactics would work—and that you would not renege on any deal made in the heat of the moment—I might almost be prepared to risk them,' she told him with pseudo-sweetness, her tone changing completely as she added in a much colder and more authoritative voice, 'But if I were in your shoes...'

'You'd do things differently?' Leo supplied for her.

'Well, if I were you I'd make sure of my facts before I started throwing accusations around.' Jodi turned round, giving him one last furious look as she told him, 'I'm not listening to any more of this.'

And then she was gone before Leo had the chance to stop her, leaving him mentally cursing both her and himself.

Why on earth hadn't he simply told her that he had found a way of keeping the factory open?

Why? Because his damned stupid male pride wouldn't let him, that was why!

By the time she had walked home, Jodi was feeling both queasy and slightly light-headed. It was because of the heat of the sun and the fact that she had not really had very much to eat, Jodi told herself firmly—to even think of allowing herself to imagine anything else was completely and utterly silly.

Silly, yes, but still somehow she couldn't stop herself

from imagining, dreading that her foolish behaviour was now going to have dire consequences.

It wasn't that she didn't like children—she did, nor even that she didn't want to be a mother and have babies herself—she did. But not yet, and most certainly not like this.

No, she wanted her babies to be planned for with love, by two people equally committed to their relationship and their children's future.

She was, she told herself, panicking unnecessarily, deliberately blowing up a small feeling of nausea into something else. Easy to tell herself that, but far harder to believe it. Guilt was a terribly powerful force!

With her imagination running away from her at full speed and sending her harrowing images of single-parenthood, it was hard to think rationally.

Even if she was pregnant, it was far too soon for her to be suffering from morning sickness, surely, and if her nausea wasn't caused by that then how could she be pregnant?

But what if she was? What if? A woman in her position, a schoolteacher, pregnant after a one-night stand! She went cold at the thought, filled with repugnance for her own behaviour. Mentally she started counting the days until she could be sure that she was safe. And in the meantime... In the meantime she would just have to try not to panic!

CHAPTER EIGHT

JODI could feel the buzz of excitement being generated by the group of parents gathered outside the school gates. Puzzled, she looked at them. Normally on a Monday parental exchanges were slightly subdued, but this morning's mood was quite obviously very upbeat—unlike her own, Jodi recognised, pausing as one of the parents called out to her.

'Have you heard the news—isn't it wonderful? I could hardly believe it when John came home on Saturday and told me that Leo Jefferson had announced he intended to keep the factory open.'

Jodi stared at her.

Leo had done that? But he had told her... Before she could sort out her confused thoughts another mother was joining in the conversation, chuckling warmly as she congratulated Jodi on her part in the previous week's demonstration at the factory.

'We were all really surprised and impressed by the way Mr Jefferson spoke up for you to the police, telling them that he had no intention of taking things any further. And then to learn that he's going to keep the factory open after all. It totally changes the way we all think about him.' She beamed, giving Jodi a look she didn't understand before continuing, 'Of course, you must have known what was going to happen before the rest of us!' Jodi's face started to burn.

The other parents were also looking at her with an unexpected degree of amused speculation, she recognised, although she had no idea why until suddenly she could hear Myra Fanshawe exclaiming vehemently, 'Well, personally I think it's absolutely disgraceful. A person in her position…a schoolteacher. A head teacher…indulging in a liaison of that nature. I must say, though, I'm not totally surprised. I've never approved of some of her teaching methods!'

Myra was talking to one of the other parents, her back to Jodi. As Jodi approached the other woman whispered something urgently to Myra, her face flushing with embarrassment.

But it seemed that her embarrassment was not shared by Myra, who tossed her head and then said even more loudly, 'Well, I'm sorry, but I don't really care if she does hear me. After all, she's the one at fault. Behaving like that… Openly spending the night in his hotel suite, and then trying to convince us all that she's Ms Virtue personified!'

Jodi felt her face burning even hotter as the group of parents surrounding Myra gave way and stood back as she approached.

Jodi's heart gave a sickening lurch as she saw the look of malicious triumph in the other woman's eyes. Myra had never liked her, she knew that. Jodi had to admit that she didn't particularly care for Myra either, but there was too much at stake here for her to be ruled by such feelings.

Reminding herself—not that she needed any reminding—of her position and her responsibilities as the school's head teacher, Jodi took a deep, calming breath and confronted the other woman.

'I assume that I am the subject of your discussion, and if that is the case—'

'You aren't going to try to deny it, I hope,' Myra interrupted her rudely before Jodi could finish speaking. 'It wouldn't do you any good if you did. Ellie, the receptionist who saw you at the hotel, both when you arrived and the next morning when you left, is my goddaughter, and she recognised you immediately from your photograph in the local paper. She couldn't believe it when she read that you had been demonstrating at the factory. Not when she knew that you'd spent the night with its owner.'

Jodi's heart sank. This was even worse than she had expected, and she could see from the varying expressions on the faces of the other parents that they were all shocked by Myra's disclosures.

What could she say in her own defence? What mitigating circumstances could she summon up to explain? Bleakly Jodi was aware that there was nothing she could say that would make the situation any better and, potentially, telling the truth would make things a whole lot worse!

'You do realise, don't you, that, given my position on the board of governors, it will be my duty to bring up the doubts your behaviour gives me as to your suitability to teach our children?'

'I haven't—'

Jodi tried to interrupt and defend herself, but Myra overrode her, stating loudly, 'And, on top of everything else, you were taken into custody by the police. It is my belief that the education authority should be told!' she said to Jodi with obvious relish. 'After all, as a parent, I have my child's moral welfare to think about,' Myra was continuing with a sanctimonious fervour that had some of the more impressionable parents watching her round-eyed. 'In your shoes…' she continued in an openly triumphant manner.

To Jodi's relief, the final bell summoning the children to their classrooms started to ring, giving her the perfect opportunity to escape from her tormentor.

From her tormentor maybe, she allowed half an hour later as she stood motionlessly staring out of the window of her small office, but not from the torment itself.

She had seen the looks—from pity right through to very unpleasant salacious curiosity—on the faces of the parents as they'd watched her reaction to Myra's disclosures. She knew that Myra had the power to make life very difficult and uncomfortable for her and for her family. The other members of the board were naturally going to be concerned about the probity and the moral standing of their school's head teacher, and, although Jodi did not think that any legal disciplinary action would be taken against her, naturally she did not relish the thought of being at odds with the governors or indeed of having her lifestyle bring disrepute on the school.

And as for Myra's remark about the education authority, well, Jodi suspected that had just been so much hot air, but she also knew that her own conscience would not allow her to stay on at the school against the wishes of the parents, or in a situation where they felt that she was not the right person to have charge of their children. Jodi's heart sank. If that was to happen…! If she was to be put in a position where she felt honour bound to step down from her post, after everything she had done, all her hard work. But what could she say in her own defence? she reminded herself bleakly. And that jibe Myra had made about her maternal concern for the moral welfare of her son had really hit a raw nerve.

Jodi's head was starting to ache. She had deliberately made herself eat a heavy breakfast this morning, just to prove to herself—not that she had needed it—that she most certainly was not suffering from the nauseous early-morning tummy of a newly pregnant woman. The meal was taking its natural toll on her now.

She felt distinctly queasy, but surely because she was so tense with anxiety and misery? She tried to reassure and comfort herself, but harrowing tales of members of her sex who had found themselves in exactly the position she was dreading kept being dredged up by her conscience to torment her. And the unfortunate thing was that she was prone to having an erratic cycle, especially when she was under stress.

Myra's comments had all but obliterated the original discomfort she had felt on learning that, contrary to what he had told her, Leo had actually decided to keep the factory open. Why had he let her accuse him like that?

It was almost lunchtime before Leo learned what was happening to Jodi.

He had been tied up with his accountants most of the morning, swiftly renegotiating finance packages to accommodate the changes he had made to his business plans for the factories he had taken over.

His bankers had shaken their heads over the discovery

that he intended to set up his own haulage and distribution business and then admitted ruefully that, being Leo, he was probably going to make a very profitable success of it.

But all morning what he'd really been thinking about, worrying about, had been Jodi and the row they had had the previous day. Why had he let her go like that?

He had a meeting at the factory, and when he arrived there he discovered that Jeremy Driscoll was waiting to see him.

Furiously angry, he confronted Leo, telling him, 'I want to collect some papers I left here, but the cretins you have left in charge have refused to allow me access to the storeroom. God knows on whose instructions.'

'On mine,' Leo told him equably.

There was a copy of the local paper on the desk, and Leo frowned as he caught sight of it and saw Jodi's photograph on the front page.

Jeremy had obviously seen it too, and he sneered as he commented, 'Little Miss Goody Two Shoes. Well, everyone's going to know what she is soon enough now.'

'What do you mean?' Leo demanded tersely as he recognised the malice glinting in Jeremy's pale blue eyes.

'What do you think I mean?' Jeremy grinned. 'She was spotted leaving your suite, creeping out of the hotel in the early hours of the morning. Good, was she?

'Well, you might have been impressed but somehow I doubt the parents of the brats she teaches are going to be when they learn what she was up to. Their head teacher, tricking her way into a man's hotel suite and not leaving until the morning…' Jeremy started to shake his head disapprovingly. 'I shouldn't be surprised if they demand her resignation.'

As he listened to him Leo's heart sank. Jeremy was too sure of himself, swaggeringly so, in fact, to simply be making a shot in the dark. Someone obviously *had* seen Jodi leaving his suite.

Leo's brain went into overdrive as he sought furiously for a way to protect her. There was only one thing he could think of doing that might help.

Fixing Jeremy with a cool, bored look, he told him calmly, 'Oh, I hardly think so; after all, what's so wrong about an engaged couple spending the night together?'

'An engaged couple?' Jeremy was staring nonplussed at him, but to Leo's relief he didn't immediately reject Leo's claim; instead he challenged, 'If that's true then why doesn't anyone know about it?'

'Because we've chosen to keep it to ourselves for the moment,' Leo responded distantly, 'not that it's any business of yours or anyone else's. Oh, and by the way,' he continued, giving Jeremy a nasty smile, 'I understand from my accountants that they've been approached by the tax authorities regarding some anomalies in the accounting system you put in place here after the fire that destroyed the previous records. Of course,' Leo continued smoothly, 'my accountants have assured the Revenue that we are prepared to give them all the help they might need.'

Miserably Jodi stared across her desk. As luck would have it, the school's parents had a meeting this evening at which she was supposed to be speaking about her plans to increase the range of extra-curricular activities provided for the children. Jodi gave a small shudder. She could guess what was going to be the hot topic of conversation at that meeting now!

And she could guess, too, just how much criticism and disapproval she was going to encounter—deservedly so, she told herself grimly.

Breaking into Leo's suite, getting drunk, falling asleep in his bed and then, as though all of that weren't enough…

She wasn't fit to be a teacher, or to hold the responsible position she did, Jodi decided wretchedly, and Myra Fanshawe had been right when she had warned Jodi that the parents would take a very dim view of what she had done.

If only that photograph of her had not appeared in the local paper. But it had, and— She tensed as she heard a soft knock on her door, her face colouring as Helen Riddings, the more senior of her co-teachers, popped her head round the door to ask uncertainly, 'Are you all right? Only…'

Only what? Jodi wondered defeatedly. Only you've heard the gossip and now you're wondering if it's true and, if it is, just what I'm going to do about it?

'I'm sorry, it's my turn for playground duty, isn't it?' Jodi answered her, avoiding the other woman's eyes, knowing perfectly well that her colleague had not really come to her office to remind her about that.

'Oh, but you haven't had any lunch,' Helen protested, obviously flustered. 'I can do the playground duty for you if you like.' She stopped and then looked acutely self-conscious as she told Jodi, 'Myra Fanshawe is in the playground with some of the other parents...'

'It's all right, Helen,' Jodi told her quietly when she broke off in embarrassment. 'I can guess what's going on. I expect that you and the other teachers will have heard the gossip by now...' Jodi could feel her courage starting to desert her.

'You don't look very well,' Helen commiserated, obviously genuinely concerned for her. 'Why don't you go home?'

Before the situation became so untenable that she had no option other than to retreat there—permanently? Was that what Helen meant? Jodi wondered bitterly.

'No, I can't do that,' she responded.

She was beginning to feel acutely ill. Gossip, especially this kind of gossip, spread like wildfire; she knew that. How long would it be before it reached the ears of her friends and family? Her cousin...his parents...her own parents...?

Jodi's stomach heaved. Her mother and father, enjoying their retirement, were on an extended trip around America, but they would not be away indefinitely. Her family were so proud of her. So proud of everything she had achieved for the school. What could she say to them when they asked her for an explanation? That she had seen Leo Jefferson in the hotel foyer and fallen immediately and helplessly in lust with him?

In lust. As Helen left her office and closed the door behind her Jodi made a small moan of self-disgust.

But it wasn't lust she felt for Leo Jefferson, was it? Lust did not affect the emotions the way her emotions had been affected. Lust did not bring a person out of their dreams at night, crying out in pain and loss because that person had discovered a cruel truth about the man they loved.

Her stomach churned even more fiercely.

She wasn't going to be sick, she wasn't. But suddenly, urgently, Jodi knew that she was!

It was tension, that was all, nothing else. Jodi assured herself later when she was on her way to take her first afternoon class.

She wondered if it was too soon to buy one of those test kits; that way she could be completely sure. Jodi flinched as she reflected on the effect it would have on the current gossip about her it she was to be observed buying a pregnancy-testing kit. No, she couldn't take such a risk!

Was it really only such a short time ago that she had been a model of virginal morality, basking in the approval of both the parents and the school authorities? And she'd been in receipt of an offer of employment from the area's most prestigious private school... She felt as though that Jodi belonged to another life! How could she have got herself into such a situation? She had heard that falling in love was akin to a form of madness.

Falling in love! Now she knew she was dangerously close to losing her grip on reality. No way did she still think she was in love with Leo Jefferson. No way!

Leo looked at his watch. He had been in meetings for the whole of the afternoon, but at last he was free.

He was acutely conscious of the fact that it might be politic for him to warn Jodi about their 'engagement', but after the way they had parted the last time they had met he doubted that trying to telephone her was going to be very successful.

School must be over for the day by now. He could drive over to the village and call on her at home, explain what had happened, tell her that once the furore had died down they could discreetly let it be known that the engagement was off.

Just the memory of the salacious look in Jeremy Driscoll's eyes when he had taunted Leo this morning about the gossip now circulating concerning Jodi was enough to make Leo feel murderous and to wish that he had the real right to protect Jodi in the way that he wanted to be able to protect her. And, so far as he was concerned, the best way to do that was for her to have his ring on her left hand—his wedding ring! He really was far more Italian than he had ever realised, he recognised grimly as he headed for his car, which reminded him—he ought to telephone his parents. The visit he had promised his mother he would make to see them again soon would have to be put back, at least until he was satisfied that Jodi was all right.

'I take it that you will be attending the meeting this evening?'

Jodi tensed warily as Myra Fanshawe stepped past the other parents grouped at the school gates to confront her.

'Only, now that you've got a wealthy fiancé to consider, I don't imagine you're going to be particularly concerned about the future of the school or its pupils, are you?'

A wealthy fiancé. Her? What on earth was Myra talking about? Jodi wondered wearily.

She couldn't remember ever feeling so drained at the end of a school day, but of course this had been no ordinary day, which no doubt explained why all she wanted to do was to go to sleep, but not until after she had had some delicious anchovies... For some reason she had been longing for some all afternoon! Which was most peculiar because they were not normally something she was very keen on!

Myra was standing in front of her now, her cold little eyes narrowing with hostility as she continued, 'I hope you don't think that just because you're engaged to Leo Jefferson it means that certain questions aren't going to be asked—by the parents if not the education authority,' she sniffed prissily. 'And—'

'Just a minute,' Jodi stopped her sharply, 'what exactly do you mean about me being engaged to Leo Jefferson?'

She was starting to feel light-headed again, Jodi recognised, her face burning hot and then cold as she wondered how on earth Myra could possibly have got hold of such an outrageous idea—and quite obviously spread it around as fast and as far as she could, Jodi guessed despairingly as she saw the other parents watching them.

'It's a little too late for you to assume either discretion or innocence now,' Myra told her disdainfully. 'Although I must say that, as a parent, I do think that someone in your position should have made more of an attempt to employ them both instead of acting in a way that could bring the school into disrepute.'

'Myra...' Jodi began grimly, and then stopped as the small knot of parents in front of the gates fell back to allow the large Mercedes to pull to a halt outside them.

'Well, here comes your fiancé,' Myra announced bitchily as Leo got out of the car. 'I just hope he doesn't think because he's bought Frampton at a ridiculous, knock-down price—virtually tricking the family into selling the business to him against their will, from what Jeremy has told us—it means that he's got any kind of position or authority locally! Jeremy was very highly thought-of by his workforce,' she continued, with such a blatant disregard for the truth that Jodi could hardly believe her ears.

Leo had reached them now, and for a reason she certainly was not going to analyse, Jodi discovered that a small part of her actually felt pleased to have him there.

Not that he had any right to be here, making a bad situation even worse by putting his hand proprietorily on Jodi's arm, before bending his head to brush his lips lightly against her cheek as he murmured into her ear, 'I'll explain when we're on our own.' Then he moved slightly away from her to say in a louder voice, 'Sorry I'm late, darling; I got held up.'

And then, without giving her an opportunity to say a word, he was guiding her towards his car, tucking her solicitously into the passenger seat, and then getting in the driver's seat beside her.

Jodi waited until she was sure that they were safely out of sight of the gathered watchers, before demanding shakily, 'Would you mind explaining to me just what is going on, and why Myra Fanshawe seems to think that we are engaged?'

'Myra Fanshawe?' Leo queried, puzzled.

'The woman with me as you drove up,' Jodi explained impatiently.

She felt tired and cross and very hungry, and the ridiculous temptation to beg Leo to stop the car so that she could lay her head on his shoulder and wallow in the cathartic pleasure of a really good cry was so strong that it was threatening to completely overwhelm her.

'She's a close friend of Jeremy Driscoll,' she offered casually, 'and—'

'Oh, is she?' Leo growled. 'Well, no doubt that explains how she knows about our engagement.'

'Our engagement?' Jodi checked him angrily. 'What engagement? We are not engaged...'

'Not officially—'

'Not in any way,' Jodi interrupted him fiercely.

'Jodi, I had no choice,' Leo told her quietly. 'Driscoll told me about the fact that you'd been seen leaving my suite early in the morning. He was...' Leo paused, not wanting to tell her just how unpleasant Jeremy's attitude and assumptions had been. 'Apparently—'

'I know what you're going to say.' Jodi stopped him hotly. 'I was seen leaving your room, so I must be some kind of fallen woman, totally unfit to teach school, to be involved with innocent children. For heaven's sake, all I've done is to go bed with you twice; that doesn't mean...'

To her own consternation her eyes filled with emotional tears, her voice becoming suspended by the sheer intensity of what she was feeling...

'Jodi, I know exactly what it does mean and what it doesn't mean,' Leo tried to reassure her. 'But that knowledge belongs only to the two of us. You do know what I'm saying, don't you?' he asked her gently.

When she made no response and instead looked studiedly away from him out of the passenger window he could see the deep pink colour burning her skin and his heart ached for her.

'I didn't think you'd particularly care for it if I were to take out a full-page advert in the local paper announcing that you were a virgin until that night in my suite.'

'That doesn't mean you have to claim that we're engaged,' Jodi protested.

'I did it to protect you,' Leo told her.

To protect her! How could he sit there and claim to want to protect her when he had already told her that he didn't want to keep their child? Or was that why he was doing this? Jodi wondered wretchedly. Was this just a cynical ploy to make her feel she could trust him, to keep her close enough to him for him to be able to control her, and act quickly, if necessary, to…?

'It isn't your responsibility to protect me.' Jodi told him fiercely.

'Maybe not in your eyes,' Leo retaliated, suddenly serious in a way that made her heart thud in pure female awareness of how very male and strong he was, and how she longed to be able to lean on that strength, and to feel she could turn to it and him for comfort and for protection and for love…

But of course she couldn't! Mustn't…

'But in mine, Jodi, I can assure you that I consider it very much my responsibility. You aren't the only one with a reputation to consider and protect, you know,' he told her. His voice was suddenly so hurtfully curt that Jodi turned to look at him—and then wished that she hadn't, as the mere sight of his profile caused a wave of helpless longing to pulse through her body, pushing every other emotion out of its way.

She must not feel like this about him, Jodi told herself in defensive panic. She must not want him, ache for him…love him…

A small sound somewhere between pain and despair constricted her throat.

'How do you think it is going to reflect on me once it becomes public knowledge that you and I—?'

'You mean, you're doing this for yourself and not for me?' Jodi challenged him.

This was more like it. Knowing that his behaviour was motivated by selfishness would surely help her to control and ultimately conquer her love for him?

'I'm doing it because right now it is the only option we have,' Leo told her firmly.

Jodi could feel herself weakening. It would be such a relief to simply let Leo take charge, to let him stand between her and the disapproval of public opinion.

To let the world at large believe that he loved her and that…

No. She could not do it. Because if she did she would be in grave danger of allowing herself to believe the same thing!

'No!' she told him fiercely, shaking her head in rejection. 'I'm not going to hide behind you, Leo, or lie, or pretend… What I did might have been wrong. Immoral in some people's eyes. But in my own eyes what would be even worse would be to lie about it. If people want to criticise or condemn me then I shall just have to accept that and be judged by them; accept the consequences of my behaviour.'

As he watched her and saw the fear fighting with the pride in her eyes Leo was filled with a mixture of admiration for her honesty and a helpless, aching tenderness for her vulnerability. She was so innocent, so naïve. He had to protect her from herself as much as from others.

As he swung his car into the drive to Ashton House he told her bluntly, 'You'll be crucified. Do you really want to throw away everything you've worked for, Jodi? The school, everything you've achieved there? Because I promise you that is what could happen.'

'There are other schools,' Jodi told him whilst she struggled to contain the pain his words were causing her.

He brought the car to a standstill and Jodi suddenly realised just where they were.

'Why have you brought me here?' she demanded indignantly. 'I wanted to go home.'

'You're my fiancée,' Leo told her silkily. 'This is your home.'

'No,' Jodi protested furiously. 'No… I…' She stopped and shook her head. 'We can't be engaged,' she told him helplessly. 'It isn't… We don't…'

'We have to be, Jodi,' Leo responded, shattering what was left of her composure by telling her, 'We can't afford not to be.'

'Take me home,' Jodi demanded wretchedly. 'To my home.' She added insistently, 'I've got a meeting tonight and if I don't go Myra Fanshawe is going to have a field-day.'

Jodi sank down onto her small sofa. The meeting had been every bit as bad as she had dreaded, with Myra

Fanshawe openly attempting to turn it into a debate on morality, plainly intent on embarrassing and humiliating Jodi just as much as she could.

Jodi had not been without her supporters, though; and several people had come up to her to congratulate her with genuine warmth on her engagement.

'It must have been very hard for both of you,' one of the parents had sympathised with her, 'with your fiancé potentially planning to close down the factory and you being committed to keeping it open. However,' she'd added with a smile, 'love, as they say, conquers all.'

Love might very well do so, Jodi reflected miserably now, but she was never likely to find out, since Leo quite plainly did not love her.

Her telephone rang, and this time, expecting Nigel, she picked up the receiver.

'You're a dark horse, aren't you?' were his opening words.

Jodi's heart sank.

'You've heard,' she guessed.

'Of course I've heard,' Nigel agreed wryly. 'The whole damned town has heard. Oh, and by the way, the parents have been on to me, wanting to know when they're going to get to meet your fiancé; I think my mother was on the phone to yours this afternoon.'

'What?' Jodi yelped in dismay. 'But I didn't want them to know...'

'What?' Nigel sounded confused.

'I mean I didn't want them to know yet,' Jodi hastily corrected herself. 'I mean I wanted to tell them myself and, what with everything happening so quickly...'

'Very quickly,' Nigel agreed with cousinly frankness

as he told her, 'I must say, I got a bit of a shock to learn that you'd spent the night with Leo at his hotel, especially in view of the fact that you treated him like public enemy number one at the dinner party.'

'Oh, Nigel…' Jodi began, and then stopped. How on earth could she explain to her cousin just what had happened? And how on earth could she explain to anyone else if she couldn't explain to Nigel?

When she had told Leo that she didn't want to involve herself in any kind of deceit or hide behind him she had meant what she had said, but now suddenly she realised that things were not quite so simple as that and that there were other people in her life whose views and feelings she had to take into account.

For several minutes after she had finished her call with Nigel she sat nibbling on her bottom lip before finally reaching for the phone.

She dialled Leo's number while her fingers trembled betrayingly.

When he answered just the sound of his voice was enough to make her stomach quiver in helpless reaction.

'It's Jodi,' she told him huskily. 'I've been thinking about what you said about our…about us being engaged and I…I agree…'

When Leo made no response her mouth went dry. What if he had changed his mind? What if he no longer cared about his own reputation or felt it was his responsibility, as he had put it, to protect hers?

And then she heard the click as the receiver was suddenly replaced and her heart lurched sickeningly. He *had* changed his mind!

Now what was she going to do?

Ten minutes later she curled herself up into her sofa in a forlorn little ball and then frowned as her front doorbell suddenly rang.

It would be Nigel again, no doubt, she decided wearily, getting up and padding barefoot to the door.

Only it wasn't Nigel, it was Leo, and as she stepped into her hallway she realised that he was carrying a bottle of champagne and two glasses.

'There's only one real way in my book an engaged couple should celebrate their commitment to one another,' Leo told her in a laconic drawl as she stared at him, 'and it involves privacy and a bed. Preferably a very large bed, and a very long period of privacy, but, since our engagement is not of the committed-for-life variety, this will have to be the alternative…'

As he finished speaking Leo looked at her, and Jodi knew that her face was burning—not with embarrassment or anger, she realised guiltily, but with the heat of the sheer longing his words had conjured up inside her.

'Of course,' Leo was suggesting softly, 'if you would prefer the first option…'

Jodi gave him an indignant look.

'What I'd prefer,' she told him, 'is not to be in this wretched situation at all.'

As she turned away from him Leo wondered what she would say if he told her just how dangerously close he was to picking her up in his arms and taking her somewhere very private and keeping her there until she was so full of the love he wanted to give her that…

That what? he asked himself in mental derision. That she would tell him that she loved him?

'How did the parents' meeting go?' he asked her

gently as he opened the champagne and poured them both a glass.

'Our engagement opened to mixed reviews,' Jodi told him wryly.

She wasn't going to tell him that Myra had informed her before she had left that she had decided it was her moral duty to inform the education authority of the situation.

'It's only a storm in a teacup.' Leo told her gently. 'Six months from now all this will be forgotten.'

That wasn't what he'd said earlier, Jodi thought, when he'd insisted that the only way to protect her job was for them to be engaged. Jodi bit her lip. Still, in six months' time Leo might have forgotten her but she would never be able to forget him.

Leo handed Jodi one of the glasses of champagne. Shaking her head, she refused to take it.

'No, I can't,' she told Leo bleakly.

To her relief he didn't press her, simply putting the glass down before asking her quietly, 'Because of the effect the cocktail at the hotel had on you? Jodi, from the smell of the jug, it contained the most lethal mixture of alcohol…'

Before he could finish Jodi was shaking her head. Oddly perhaps, in the circumstances, that had not been her reason for refusing the champagne.

'It isn't that,' she told him hollowly. 'It's that I hate having to pretend like this,' she told him simply. 'I abhor the deceit, and it just seems wrong somehow to celebrate in such a traditional and romantic way what is, after all, just a pretence…a fiction—'

'Jodi!'

Her honesty, so direct and unexpected, had brought a dangerous lump of emotion to Leo's throat. She looked so sad, so grave-eyed, so infinitely lovable that he wanted to take hold of her and...

'It doesn't...'

'Please, I don't want to discuss it any more.' Jodi told him, getting up and moving restlessly around the room.

She knew what he had been going to say. He had been going to say that under the circumstances their dishonesty didn't matter, and perhaps it didn't—to him, but it mattered to her. Most of all because there was something unbearably hurtful...something that was almost a desecration, about them cynically using a custom that should be so special and meaningful, and reserved only for those who truly loved each other and believed in that love, for their own practical ends.

'I...I'd like you to go now,' she told him chokily.

For a moment Leo hesitated. She looked so vulnerable, so fragile that he wanted to stay with her, to be with her, and she looked pale and tired as well...

Frowningly Leo checked and studied her again.

'Jodi. I know we've already been through this, but...if there is any chance that you could be wrong and you are pregnant, then I—'

'I am not pregnant,' Jodi interrupted him sharply.

If she had been wondering if perhaps she had misjudged him, her defences weakened by his unexpected sensitivity towards her and the situation she was in, then he had just given her the proof that she had not, she recognised bitterly.

If, too, she had been foolishly reading some kind of selfless and caring emotion into his arrival at her house tonight, and the things he had said to her, then she was certainly being made sharply aware of her error.

Of course there was only one reason he was here, only one reason he was concerned, and only one person he was concerned for! And that person certainly wasn't her, or the child he quite obviously did not want her to have.

'I'm tired,' she told him flatly. 'And I want you to go...'

As she spoke she was already heading for the front door.

Leo followed her.

As he got back in his car, he wondered what he had hoped to gain by his actions. Had he really thought that the simple act of calling to see her, bringing her champagne so that they could celebrate their fictitious engagement together, was in any way going to change her lack of love for him? How could it?

He might be a fool, he decided determinedly as he drove back to Ashton House, but he was still an honourable man and he damned well intended to make sure that both Jodi and her reputation were protected for just so long as they needed to be, whether she wanted it or not. As of now they were an engaged couple in the eyes of the outside world. And soon she would be wearing his ring to prove it!

CHAPTER NINE

UNABLE to stop herself, Jodi stared at the discreet, but flawlessly brilliant solitaire diamond engagement ring she was wearing.

She had protested long and loud against Leo's decision to buy her a ring, but he had refused to give in. In the end she had been the one to do that, partially out of sheer weariness and partially out of a cowardice she was loath to admit to.

Her aunt and uncle, Nigel's parents, had invited her and Leo to have dinner with them, and Jodi had known, as indeed Leo had warned her, that, being of an older generation, they would expect to see a newly engaged woman wearing a ring.

And it had been because of that and only because of that that she had allowed Leo to drive her to the city and buy her the diamond she was now wearing on her left hand.

At first she had tried to insist that she should wear something inexpensive and fake, but Leo had been so angered by her suggestion that she had been shocked into giving in.

She hadn't been allowed to know the price of the ring Leo had finally chosen for her. She had tried to opt for the smallest diamond the jeweller in the exclusive shop had shown her but Leo had simply insisted that she try on several rings before announcing that the one he liked best was the solitaire she was now wearing.

His choice had been another shock to Jodi, because it was in fact the very ring she would have chosen herself—under different circumstances. Now, as she sat next to him in his car, she couldn't help touching it a little self-consciously as the diamond caught the light and threw out a dazzling sparkle.

She wasn't exactly looking forward to this evening's dinner, much as she loved her aunt and uncle. They were a very traditional couple, especially her aunt, who was bound to ask all manner of difficult questions.

'You didn't have to do this,' she told Leo awkwardly as she gave him directions to their home. 'I could have come up with an excuse. After all, with the takeover...'

It was all over the village now that Jeremy Driscoll was being investigated by the revenue authorities, but even that gossip had not been enough to silence Myra Fanshawe's repeated references to her concern over Jodi's behaviour.

'You want to speak to Mr Jefferson?' Leo's new secretary at the factory asked the woman caller who had asked to speak to Leo. The woman had explained that she hadn't been able to get through to him on his mobile and that she hadn't heard from him in several days.

'Oh, I'm sorry, but he isn't here at the moment. And I expect he's switched off his mobile, because he's gone to meet his fiancée.'

On the other end of the line, Leo's mother, Luisa Jefferson, almost dropped her receiver.

'His fiancée,' she repeated. 'Oh, well, yes…of course.'

'Shall I tell him you called?' Leo's secretary asked her helpfully.

'Er—no…that won't be necessary,' Luisa informed her.

Replacing the receiver, she went in search of her husband, whom she found seated on a sun lounger beside their pool.

'I have to go to England to see Leonardo,' she informed him.

The evening had gone surprisingly well. Leo had laughed obligingly at her uncle's jokes and praised her aunt's cooking with such a genuineness that it was plain that they were both already ready to welcome him with open arms into the family.

Jodi, with the benefit of far more objectivity at her disposal, watched the proceedings with pardonable cynicism.

'So,' Jodi heard her aunt asking archly, once they were in her sitting room with their after-dinner coffee. 'what about the wedding? Have you made any plans as yet?'

'No—'

'Yes—'

As they both spoke at once her aunt looked from Leo's smiling face to Jodi's set one with an understandably baffled expression.

'We've only just got engaged,' Jodi defended her denial.

'I'd marry Jodi tomorrow if she'd agree,' Leo told her

aunt with a wicked, glinting smile in Jodi's direction that made her want to scream. He was enjoying this. She could tell.

'Well, of course Jodi will want to wait until her parents return,' her aunt said lovingly, before asking, 'And what about your parents, Leo?'

'I want to take Jodi out to Italy to meet them just as soon as I can,' Leo responded truthfully, 'but I already know that they will love her as much as I do.' And then, before Jodi could guess what he intended to do, he leaned towards her, taking one of her hands and enfolding it tenderly between both of his before bending his head to brush his mouth against hers.

Jodi could feel the quivering, out-of-control wanting begin deep down inside her the moment he touched her; it shocked and frightened her, and it made her feel very angry as well. She felt angry with Leo for making her love him, and angry with herself too, and yet she still couldn't stop herself from closing her eyes and wishing that all of this was real; that he did love her; that their futures really lay together.

Jodi's aunt and uncle said goodbye to them at their front door. Leo had placed his arm around Jodi as they walked to the door, and he kept it there whilst they walked to the car, even though it was parked out of direct sight of the house.

'You can let go of me now,' Jodi told him as they reached the car. 'No one can see us.'

'What if I don't want to let go of you?' Leo demanded softly.

There was just enough moonlight for Jodi to be able

to see the hot glint of desire that glittered in his eyes as he looked down at her.

Shakily she backed up against the car, her heart hammering against her ribs—but not with fear.

'Leo!' she protested, but he was already sliding his hands slowly up over the bare flesh of her arms. His touch made her tremble with desire, her emotions so tightly strung that she was afraid of what she might do. If just the casual caress of his hands could make her feel like this...

But she was so hungry for him. So very, very hungry!

'We're engaged,' Leo breathed against her ear. 'Remember...we're allowed to do this, expected to...and, God knows, I want to!' he told her, his voice suddenly changing and becoming so fiercely charged with sensuality that it made Jodi shiver all over again.

'But our engagement isn't real,' she told him.

'It may not be, but this most certainly is...' Leo growled.

And then he was holding her, one large hand on her waist, whilst the other cupped her face, tilting it, holding it. Jodi held her breath as she felt him looking at her, and then he was bending his head, and his mouth was on hers and...

When had she lifted her own hand towards his jaw? When had she parted her mouth for the hot, silent passion of his kiss? When had she closed that final tiny distance between them, her free hand gripping his arm, her fingers digging into its muscle as the ache inside her pounded down her defences?

'What is it about you that makes me feel like this?' Leo was demanding thickly, but Jodi knew that the words, raw with longing, helpless in the face of so much desire, might just as well have been her own.

She knew too that if Leo was to take her home with him now there was no way she would be able to resist the temptation he was offering her. Right now she wanted him more than she wanted her pride, her self-respect, or her sanity!

'Right now,' she heard Leo telling her thickly, 'I could…'

An owl hooted overhead, startling them both, and abruptly Leo was moving back from her, leaving her feeling cold and alone as he turned to unlock the car doors.

Jodi stared mutely at the package she was holding in her hand. She had bought it when she had been in the city with Leo, the day he had taken her there to get her engagement ring. She had seen the chemist's shop and had managed to slip away to get what she had begun to fear she needed.

That had been well over three weeks ago now and… Reluctantly she turned the package over and read the instructions. It was just a precaution, she told herself firmly, that was all.

It was practically impossible that her suspicions were anything more than simple guilty anxiety. Sometimes odd things happened to bodies, especially when their owners were under the kind of stress she was under right now.

Myra had informed her that her committee had felt that they had no option other than to report their concerns over her behaviour to the education authority, and that was exactly what they had done.

Jodi had already had to undergo an extremely difficult and worrying telephone interview, and now she was waiting to see what they were going to do.

At best, she would simply get a black mark against her for having been reported, and at worst... Jodi didn't want to think about what the worst-case scenario could be.

Jodi was under no delusions about the seriousness of the situation she was in, but right now...

She looked unhappily at the pregnancy-testing kit she was holding. She didn't really need to do it, did she? After all, it was only a matter of a few days late—well, a week or so—and she was one hundred per cent sure that that unwelcome feeling of nausea she had been experiencing recently was simply nerves and tension.

And the craving for anchovies?

She was careful about her health and followed a low-fat, low-salt diet. Her body had decided that it needed salt, obviously. Obviously!

Taking a deep breath, Jodi took the kit out of its packet. It was going to show negative, she knew that. She knew it.

Positive. Jodi stared at the testing kit, unable and unwilling to accept the result it was showing. Her hand shook as she picked it up for the tenth time and stared at it.

It must be wrong. A faulty kit, or she had done something wrong. Panic began to fill her. She couldn't be pregnant. She couldn't be!

Leo's baby! She was going to have Leo's baby! Why on earth was she smiling? Jodi wondered in disbelief as she saw her reflection in her bathroom mirror.

This was quite definitely not smiling territory...

Downstairs she heard her post coming through the letterbox. The school term had finally come to an end, so she did not have to rush to get to work. She finished dressing and went downstairs, collecting her letters on the way.

There was a card from her parents, and a whole bunch of unsolicited trash mail.

Jodi had to sit down before she could bring herself to look at it. Her parents. No need to ask herself how they would feel about what had happened. There would be gossip, there was bound to be, and she knew that life as an unmarried mother was not the life they had envisaged for her or for their grandchild. If she was honest it was not the life she had ever envisaged for herself either. Jodi's throat felt tight and dry.

She had asked her aunt and uncle not to say anything about her engagement to her parents if they spoke to them, explaining—quite truthfully—that she wanted to tell them herself, in person.

Then, knowing that they weren't due home for another two months at least, she had convinced herself that she had plenty of time to get her life back to some kind of normality before their return, but now...!

Her parents would love her and support her no matter what she did, she knew that, and her baby, their grandchild, no matter how unconventional its conception, would be welcomed and loved. But there would be gossip and disapproval, and, with Leo continuing to be a presence locally through the factory, Jodi knew there was no way that she could stay. How could she? How could she inflict such a situation on her family, and as for her baby...how could she allow him or her to grow up suffering the humiliation of knowing that he or she had been rejected by their father?

No, life would be much easier for all those she loved if she simply moved away.

After all, she decided proudly, it wasn't as though it was her teaching skills that were in question.

And as for the fact that she would be a single mother, well, a hundred or more miles away, just who was going to be concerned or interested in the malicious criticism of Myra Fanshawe?

'Mother!'

Stunned, Leo stared into the familiar face of his very unexpected visitor as he answered his front doorbell. He had told his parents that he had moved to a rented property in Frampton and that he would be living there until he had sorted out all the complications with the business. He knew he had not been able to keep his promise to go and visit his parents again, in Italy, but he had certainly not expected to have his mother turn up on his doorstep.

'Where's Dad?' he asked her, frowning as he watched her taxi disappearing down his drive.

'I have come on my own,' his mother told him. 'I cannot stay more than a few days,' she added, 'but I am sure if we apply ourselves that will be sufficient time for me to meet your fiancée.'

Leo, who had been in the act of picking up his mother's case, suddenly straightened up to look at her.

Several responses flashed son-like through his brain, but his mother was his mother, and one very astute woman, as he had had over thirty years to find out and appreciate.

'I think you'd better come inside,' he told her steadily as he took hold of her arm.

'I think I'd better,' his mother agreed wryly, pausing only to tell him, 'This house is a very good family house, Leonardo; it is well built and strong. Children will grow very well here, and I like the garden, although it needs much work. Is she a gardener, this fiancée of yours? I hope so, for a woman who nourishes her plants will nourish her husband and her children.'

His mother was the only person in the world who called him Leonardo with that particular emphasis on the second syllable of his name, Leo reflected as he ushered her into the hallway and saw her glance thoughtfully at the vase of flowers Jodi had arranged on the hall table earlier in the week.

Leo had taken her home with him prior to visiting her aunt and uncle so that he could drop off some business papers. His telephone had rung, and the consequent call had taken some time, and when he had finally rejoined her he had discovered that she had collected some wind-blown flowers from the garden and arranged them in a vase.

'It seems such a shame to just let them die unappreciated and unloved,' she had told him defensively.

'So, she is a home-maker, this fiancée of yours,' his mother pronounced, suddenly very Italian as she subjected Jodi's handiwork to a critical maternal examination. 'Does she cook for you?'

'Mamma!' Leo sighed, leading her into the kitchen. 'There is something that you need to know…and it is going to take quite some time for me to tell you.'

'There is,' Luisa Jefferson informed her son firmly, 'only one thing I need to know and it will take you very little time to tell me. Do you love her?'

For a moment she thought that he wasn't going to reply. He was a man, after all, she reminded herself ruefully, not a boy, but then he grimaced and pushed his hair back off his face in a gesture that reminded her of her own husband before he admitted, 'Unfortunately, yes, I do.'

'Unfortunately?' she queried delicately.

'There is a problem,' Leo told her.

His mother's unexpected arrival was a complication he had not foreseen, but now that she was here he was discovering to his own amusement and with a certain sense of humility that he actually wanted to talk to her about Jodi, to share with her not just his discovery of his love for Jodi but also his confusion and concern.

'In love there is always a problem,' his mother responded humorously. 'If there is not then it is not love. So, tell me what your particular problem is… Her father does not like you? That is how a father is with his daughter. I remember my own father—'

'Mamma, I haven't met Jodi's father yet, and anyway…I have told you that I love Jodi, but what I have not told you yet is that she does not love me.'

'Not love you? But you are engaged, and I must say, Leonardo, that I did not enjoy learning of your engagement from your secretary; however—'

'Mamma please,' Leo interrupted her firmly. 'Let me explain.'

When he did Leo was careful to edit his story so that his mother would not, as he had initially done, jump to any unfair or judgemental conclusions about Jodi, but he could tell that she was not entirely satisfied with his circumspect rendition of events.

'You love her and she does not love you, but she has agreed to become engaged to you to protect her reputation, since by accident she fell asleep in your hotel suite and was seen leaving early in the morning?'

Her eyebrows lifted in a manner that conveyed a whole range of emotions, most of which made Leo's heart sink.

'I am very interested to meet this fiancée of yours, Leonardo.'

Leo drew in his breath.

'Well, as to that, I cannot promise that you will,' he began. 'I have to go to London on business this afternoon, and I had planned to stay there for several days. You could come with me if you wish and do some shopping,' he offered coaxingly.

His mother gave him an old-fashioned look.

'I live in Italy now, Leonardo. We have Milan. I do not need to shop. No, whilst you are in London I shall stay here and wait for you to return,' she pronounced. 'Where does she live, this fiancée of yours?' she asked determinedly.

Leo sighed.

'She lives here in Frampton. Mamma, I know you mean well,' he told her gently. 'But please, I would ask you not to...to...'

'To interfere?' she supplied drily for him. 'I am your mother, Leonardo, and I am Italian…'

'I understand,' Leo told her gently. 'But I hope you will understand that, since I know that Jodi does not love me, it can only cause me a great deal of humiliation and unwanted embarrassment if it was to be brought to her attention that I love her, and quite naturally I do not wish to subject either of us to those emotions, which means…' He took a deep breath. 'What I have told you, Mamma, is for your ears only, and I would ask that it remains so, and that you do not seek Jodi out to discuss any of this with her. I do not want her to be upset or embarrassed in any way, by anyone.'

For a moment he thought that she was going to refuse, and then she took a deep breath herself and agreed.

'I shall not seek her out.'

'Thank you.'

As he leaned forward to kiss her Leo heard his mother complaining, 'When I prayed that you would fall in love I did not mean for something like this to happen!'

'You want grandchildren, I know.' Leo smiled, struggling to lighten the mood of their conversation.

'I want grandchildren,' his mother agreed, 'but what I want even more is to see you sharing your life with the person you love; I want to see your life being enriched and made complete by the same kind of love your father and I have shared. I want for you what every mother wants for her child,' she told him fiercely, her eyes darkening with maternal protection and love. 'I want you to be happy.'

*   *   *

His mother couldn't want those things she had described to him any more than he wanted them for himself, Leo acknowledged a couple of hours later as he drove towards Frampton *en route* for London. He had left his mother busily dead-heading roses, whilst refusing to listen to any suggestion he tried to make that, since he could not say categorically when he would be back, she might as well return home to Italy.

In the village the temptation to turn the car towards Jodi's cottage was so strong that Leo found he was forced to grip the steering wheel to control it.

His life would never be happy now, he reflected morosely.

Not without Jodi in it. Not without her love, her presence, her warmth; not without her!

Jodi stared at her computer screen, carefully reading the resignation letter she had been working on for the last three hours. Now it was done, and there was nothing to stop her from printing it off and posting it, but somehow she could not bring herself to do so—not yet.

She got up and paced the floor, and then on a sudden impulse she picked up her keys and headed for the door.

It was a beautiful, warm summer's day, and the gardens of the cottages that lined her part of the village street overflowed with flowers, creating an idyllic scene.

Normally just the sight of them would have been enough to lift her spirits and make her think how fortunate she was to live where she did and to be the person she was, a person who had a job she loved, a family she loved, a life she loved.

But not a man she loved... The man she loved... And not the job she loved either—soon. But, though the school and her work were important to her, they did not come anywhere near matching the intensity of the love she had for Leo.

Leo. Busy with her thoughts, Jodi had walked automatically towards the school.

There was a bench opposite it, outside the church, and Jodi sat down on it, looking across at the place that meant so much to her and which she had worked so hard for.

She was not so vain that she imagined that there were no other teachers who could teach as ably, if not more so, as she had done herself, but would another teacher love the school the way she had done? Would another woman love Leo the way she did?

Her eyes filled with tears, and as she reached hurriedly into her bag for a tissue she was aware of a woman sitting down on the bench next to her.

'Are you all right, only I could not help but notice that you are crying?'

The woman's comment caught Jodi off guard. It was, not, after all, a British national characteristic to comment on a stranger's grief, no matter how sympathetic towards them and curious about them one might be.

Proudly Jodi lifted her head and turned to look at the woman.

'I'm fine, thank you,' she told her, striving to sound both cool and dismissive, but to her horror fresh tears were filling her eyes, spilling down over her cheeks, and her voice had begun to wobble alarmingly. Jodi knew that any moment now she was going to start howling like a child with a skinned knee.

'No, you aren't. You are very upset and you are also very angry with me for saying so, but sometimes it can help to talk to a stranger,' the other woman was telling her gently, before adding, 'I saw you looking at the school…'

'Yes,' Jodi acknowledged. 'I…I teach there. At least, I did…but now…' She bit her lip.

'You have decided to leave,' her interlocuter guessed. 'You have perhaps fallen in love and are to move away and you are crying because you know you will miss this very beautiful place.'

Although her English was perfect, Jodi sensed that there was something about her questioner that said that she was not completely English. She must be a visitor, someone who was passing through the area, someone she, Jodi, would never, ever see again.

Suddenly, for some inexplicable reason Jodi discovered that she did want to talk to her, to unburden herself, and to seek if not an explanation for what was happening to her, then at least the understanding of another human being. Something told her that this woman would be understanding. It was written in the warmth of her eyes and the encouragement of her smile.

'I am in love,' Jodi admitted, 'but it is not… He…the man I love…he doesn't love me.'

'No? Then he is a fool,' the other woman pronounced firmly. 'Any man who does not love a woman who loves him is a fool.' She gave Jodi another smile and Jodi realised that she was older than she had first imagined from her elegant appearance, probably somewhere in her late fifties.

'Why does he not love you? Has he told you?'

Jodi found herself starting to smile.

'Sort of… He has indicated that…'

'But you are lovers?' the woman pressed Jodi with a shrewdness and perspicacity that took Jodi's breath away.

She could feel her colour starting to rise as she admitted, 'Yes, but…but he didn't… It was at my instigation… I…' She stopped and bit her lip again. There were some things she could just not bring herself to put into words, but her companion, it seemed, had no such hang-ups.

'You seduced him!'

She sounded more amused than shocked, and when Jodi looked at her she could actually see that there was laughter in the other woman's dark eyes.

'Well…I…sort of took him by surprise. I'd fallen asleep in his bed, you see, and he didn't know I was there, and when I woke up and realised that he was and…' Jodi paused. There was something cathartic about what she was doing, about being able to confide in another person, being able to explain for the first time just what she had felt and why she had felt it.

'I'd seen him earlier in the hotel foyer,' she began in a low voice. 'I didn't know who he was, not then, but I…'

She stopped.

'You were attracted to him?' the other woman offered helpfully.

Gratefully Jodi nodded.

'Yes,' she agreed vehemently. 'He affected me in a way that no other man had ever done. I just sort of looked at him and...' Her voice became low and strained. 'I know it sounds foolish, but I believe I fell in love with him there and then at first sight...and I suppose when I woke up and found myself in bed with him my...my body must have remembered how I'd felt then, earlier, and.... But he...well, he thought that I was there because... And then later, when he realised the truth, he told me... He asked me...' Her voice tailed off. 'I should never have done what I did, and I felt so ashamed.'

'For falling in love?' the older woman asked her, giving a small shrug. 'Why should you be ashamed of that? It is the most natural thing in the world.'

'Falling in love might be,' Jodi agreed, 'but my behaviour, the way I...' Jodi shook her head primly and had to swallow hard as she tried to blink away her threatening tears.

Her companion, though, was not deterred by her silence and demanded determinedly, 'So, you have met a man with whom you have fallen in love. You say he does not love you, but are you so sure?'

'Positive,' Jodi insisted equally determinedly.

'And now you sit here weeping because you cannot bear the thought of your life without him,' the older woman guessed.

'Yes, because of that, and...and for other reasons,' Jodi admitted.

'Other reasons?'

Jodi drew an unsteady breath.

'When...after...after he had realised that I was not as

he had first imagined, well, when he realised the truth
about me he warned me that if...if by some mischance
I...there should be...repercussions from our intimacy
then he would expect me to...to...'

Jodi bit down on her lip and looked away as fresh
tears welled in her eyes.

'I told myself that it was impossible for me to love a
man like that, a man who would callously destroy the
life of his child. How could I love him?'

She shook her head in bewilderment, whilst her companion demanded in a disbelieving voice, 'I cannot believe what you are saying. It is impossible; unthink-
able...'

'I can assure you that it is the truth,' Jodi insisted
shakily. 'I didn't want to believe it myself, but he told
me. He said categorically that something would have to
be arranged. Of course, then I really did believe that it
was impossible that I could be—but now...'

As Jodi wrapped her arms protectively around her still
slender body her companion questioned sharply, 'You
are pregnant? You are to have...this man's child?'

Numbly Jodi nodded. 'Yes. And I am also facing an
enquiry because I was seen leaving his hotel suite, and
other things. And, as a head teacher, it is of course expected that I should... That was why he said we should
get engaged, because of the gossip and to protect me.'

As she spoke Jodi raised her left hand, where Leo's
diamond glistened in the sunlight nearly as brightly as
Jodi's own falling tears. 'But how can he offer to protect
me and yet want to destroy his own child?'

'What will you do?' the other woman was asking her
quietly.

Jodi drew a deep breath.

'I plan to move away and start a fresh life somewhere else.'

'Without telling your lover about his child?'

After everything she, Jodi, had told her, how could she sound so disapproving? Jodi wondered.

'How can I tell him when he has already told me that he doesn't want it? "Something will have to be arranged"—that is what he said to me, and I can imagine what kind of arrangement he meant. But I would rather die myself than do anything to hurt my baby.' Jodi was getting angry now, all her protective maternal instincts coming to the fore.

She had no idea how long she had been sitting on the bench confiding in this stranger, but now she felt so tired and drained that she longed to go home and lie down.

As she got up she gave her unknown companion a tired smile.

'Thank you for listening to me.' She turned to go, but as she did so the other woman stood up too, and to Jodi's shock took hold of her in a warm embrace, hugging her almost tenderly.

'Have courage,' she told her. 'All will be well. I am sure of it.'

As she smiled comfortingly at her, Jodi had the oddest feeling that there was something about the woman that was somehow familiar, but that, of course, was ridiculous. Jodi knew that she had never seen her before.

CHAPTER TEN

'LEONARDO, you are to drive back to Frampton right now.'

'Mamma,' Leo protested.

'Right now, Leonardo!' Luisa Jefferson insisted. 'And before you do, could you please explain to me how it is that poor Jodi believes that you wish not only to deny yourself as a father the child you have created with her, but that you wish to deny it the right to life as well?'

'What…what child? Jodi told me there would be no child.'

'And she told me that there will be, not that I needed telling; I could see it in her eyes…her face. You have hurt her very badly. She truly believes that you do not love her and she is hurting because she thinks she loves a man who would destroy her child.'

'I cannot understand how she could possibly think that!' Leo protested. 'I would never—'

'I know that, of course,' his mother interrupted him, 'but your Jodi, it seems, does not. ''Something will have to be arranged'', is apparently what you told her.'

'What…? Yes…of course…but I meant…I meant that if she was pregnant we would have to get married,' Leo told his mother grimly. 'How on earth could she interpret that as…?'

'She is the one you should be speaking to, Leonardo,

173

and not me. And you had better be quick. She plans to leave, and once she does…'

'I'm on my way,' Leo announced. 'If you dare to say anything to her until I get there you will be banned from seeing your grandchild until he or she is at least a day old.'

When she replaced her telephone receiver Luisa Jefferson was smiling beatifically.

Picking it up again, she dialled the number of her home in Italy. When her husband, Leo's father, answered she greeted him, 'Hello, Grandpapa!'

'Oh, come on, Jodi, I'm starving and I hate going out for dinner on my own.'

'But, Nigel, I'm tired,' Jodi had protested when Nigel had rung her unexpectedly, demanding that she go out to eat with him, 'and surely you could ask one of your many girlfriends.'

But in the end she had given in and she had even managed not to protest when, having picked her up in his car, he had suddenly realised that he must have dropped his wallet on her footpath and gone back to pick it up.

Now, though, at barely ten o'clock, she was exhausted, and yawning, and she couldn't blame Nigel for glancing surreptitiously at his watch.

She hadn't been the most entertaining of companions. Even so, his brisk, 'Right, let's go,' after he had checked his watch a second time made her blink a little.

'Don't you want to finish your coffee?' she asked him.

'What? Oh, no…I can see you're tired,' he offered.

He had been in an odd mood all evening, Jodi recognised, on edge and avoiding looking directly at her. But she was too tired to ask him what was wrong, instead allowing him to bustle her out into the car park and into his car.

Once they reached her house, Jodi asked him if he wanted to come in, but rather to her surprise he shook his head.

As she heard him drive away Jodi decided that she might as well go straight upstairs to bed.

In Jodi's sitting room the light from her computer screen lit up the small space around it, but Jodi was too exhausted to bother glancing into the room, and so she didn't see the smiling babies tumbling in somersaults all over her computer screen around the large typed message that read, 'I love ya, baby, and your mamma too!'

Once upstairs, she went straight to the bathroom, cleaning off her make-up and showering before padding naked into the darkened bedroom she was too familiar with to need to switch on the light.

She was already virtually asleep before she even pulled back the duvet and crawled into the longed-for comfort of her bed—the good old-fashioned king-size bed that almost filled the room and which Nigel had wickedly insisted on buying her as a cousinly moving-in gift. It was a bed that no one other than her had ever slept in—though someone was quite definitely sleeping in it now!

It was a someone she would have known anywhere, even without the benefit of being able to see his face. She would have known him simply by his scent, by the subtle air of Leo-ness that enfolded her whenever she was in his presence.

Leo! Leo was here, fast asleep in her bed! No, that just wasn't possible! She was going mad. She was daydreaming…fantasising!

'Mmm.' Jodi gasped as a decidedly realistic pair of warm arms wrapped themselves firmly around her body, imprisoning it against their owner's wonderfully familiar maleness.

'Leo!' Jodi whispered his name weakly, her voice shot through with the rainbow colours of what she was feeling.

'How could you possibly believe that I don't love you?' she heard him demanding thickly. 'I'm mad about you! Crazily, insanely, irredeemably and forever in love with you. I thought you were the one who didn't love me. But then they do say that pregnancy affects a woman's ability to reason logically…'

'Leo!' Jodi protested, her voice even weaker. She couldn't take in what was happening and, even more importantly, had no idea how it had come about. 'How? What?' she began, but Leo was in no mood to answer questions.

His lips were feathering distracting little kisses all along her jaw, her throat, her neck. He was whispering words of love and praise in her ear; he was smoothing a tender hand over the still flat plane of her belly, whilst his voice thickened openly with emotion as he whispered to her, 'How could you think I didn't want our child, Jodi?'

She tried to answer him but the seeking urgency of his mouth on hers prevented her, and, anyway, what did questions, words matter when there was this, and Leo, and the wonderful private world of tender loving they were creating between them?

'The first time we met you stole your way into my bed and my heart,' Leo said to her as he touched her with gentle, adoring hands, the true extent of his passion only burning through when he kissed her mouth. 'And there hasn't been a single day, a single hour since then when I haven't ached for you, longed for you,' he groaned. 'Not a single minute when my love for you hasn't tormented and tortured me!'

Jodi could see as well as feel the tension pulsing through his nerve-endings as he reined in his sensual hunger for her.

'Now it's my turn,' he told her. 'Thanks to Nigel, I have stolen my way into your bed, and I warn you, Jodi, I do not intend to leave it until I have stolen my way into your heart as well, and heard from your own lips that you intend to let me stay there, in your heart, in your life and the life of our child—for ever!'

'For ever,' Jodi whispered back in wonder as she touched the damp stains on his face that betrayed the intensity of his emotions.

'I might have thought that loving you was torture,' Leo told her rawly, 'but now I know that real torture would be to lose you. Do you know what it was like finding you in my bed, having you reach out and touch me, love me?' Leo was groaning achingly. 'Shall I show you?'

Hadn't her mother always warned her against the danger of playing with fire?

Right now, did she care?

'Show me!' she encouraged him boldly.

She could hear the maleness in his voice as well as feel it in his body as he told her triumphantly, 'Right.'

They made love softly and gently, aware of and awed by their role as new parents-to-be, and then fiercely and passionately as they claimed for themselves the right to be lovers for themselves.

They made love in all the ways Jodi had dreamed in her most private and secret thoughts—and then in some ways she had never imagined.

And then, as it started to become light, after Leo had told her over and over how much he loved her, how much he loved both of them, and insisted that she tell him that she returned his feelings, Jodi demanded, 'Explain to me what has happened... How...?' She stopped and shook her head in mute bewilderment. 'It's almost as though a fairy godmother has waved her wand and...'

Propping himself up one elbow, Leo looked tenderly down at her.

'That was no fairy godmother,' he quipped ruefully. 'That was my mother!'

'What?' Jodi sat bolt upright in bed, taking the duvet with her, only momentarily diverted by the magnificent sight of Leo's naked body. Long enough, though, to heave a blissful sigh of pleasure and run her fingertip lazily down the length of him, before finally playfully teasing it through the silky thickness of his body hair whilst watching with awed fascination as his body showed an unexpectedly vigorous response to her attentions.

'Don't go there,' Leo warned her humorously. 'Not unless you mean it.'

Hastily removing her hand, Jodi insisted, 'I want to hear what's been going on.'

Leo heaved a sigh of mock-disappointment.

'My mother flew over from Italy to see me. She'd heard about our engagement from my new secretary and not unnaturally, I suppose, given the nature of mothers, she decided that she wanted to meet my fiancée—the girl who had answered her prayers and those of the village wise woman, whose skills she had commissioned on my behalf. No, don't ask, not yet,' he warned Jodi, shaking his head.

'She wanted to know all about you, and I naturally obliged—well, up to a point. I told her that I'd fallen totally and completely in love with you,' he admitted to Jodi, his voice and demeanour suddenly wholly serious. 'And I told her too that you did not return my feelings. As you know, I had to go to London on business, so I invited her to go with me but she refused. She said she preferred to stay where she was until she was due to take up her return flight. I had my suspicions then, knowing her as I do, and so I made her promise that she would not under any circumstances attempt to seek you out— and she promised me that she wouldn't, but it seems from what she has told me that fate intervened.

'She had gone for a walk in the village, when, as she put it, she saw a young woman in distress. Naturally she wanted to help, so she sat down beside you and—'

'That was your mother?' Jodi interrupted. Now she began to understand!

'I felt that there was something familiar about her,' she admitted, 'but I just couldn't put my finger on what it was.

'Mmm.' She smiled lovingly as Leo broke off from his explanations to kiss her with slow thoroughness. 'Mmm...' she repeated. 'Go on.'

'With what?' Leo teased her. 'The kisses or the explanation?'

'Both!' Jodi answered him promptly.

'But the rest of the explanation first, please, otherwise...'

Laughing, Leo continued, 'Just as soon as she had left you she rang me in London, demanding to know what on earth I had said to you to give you the impression that I wouldn't want our child! Jodi...' Gravely Leo looked at her, his eyes dark with pain. 'How could you have thought that I...?'

'You said something would have to be arranged,' Jodi defended herself firmly.

'Yes, but the arrangement I had in mind was not a visit to—' He broke off, so patently unable to even say the words that Jodi instinctively wrapped her arms tightly around him, as filled with a desire to protect him as she had been to protect their unborn child.

'The place I had in mind for you to visit was a church so that we could be married,' Leo told her hoarsely. 'That was what I was talking about. Even if I had not loved you I could never, would never... Thank heavens my mother knows me better than you seem to! Still, at least that puts us on an equal footing now. I originally misjudged you and now you have misjudged me, and, that being the case, I suggest that we draw a line beneath it and start again.'

He took a deep breath. 'I love you, Jodi Marsh, and I want to marry you.'

Jodi began to smile.

'I love you too, Leo Jefferson,' she responded, 'and I want to marry you...'

'Now, getting back to the matter of those kisses...' Leo told her wickedly as he drew her back down against his body, and rolled her gently beneath him.

Several hours later, Jodi smiled a very special smile to herself. 'And so Nigel left his key for you to find under the flowerpot by the front door?' she questioned Leo as she licked the jam from her toast off her fingers and looked across the bedroom at him as he walked out of the bathroom, freshly showered, smiling as he watched her eating her toast hungrily.

'Yes; he took a considerable amount of persuading, though, and he was terrified that you might suspect that something was going on.'

'I probably would have done if I hadn't been so tired,' Jodi admitted.

Watching her, Leo could feel his love for her filling him. It had been a tremendous risk, short-circuiting things by installing himself in her bed, but thankfully it had worked, allowing them to talk openly and honestly to one another.

As Jodi finished her late breakfast he reached for her again, drawing her towards him, burying his face against her body before wrapping his arms around her and kissing her tenderly.

When his mobile rang he cursed and reached for it, starting to switch it off and then stopping as he murmured to Jodi, 'It's my mother.'

'Hello, Mamma.' He answered the call and from

where she was standing Jodi could hear his mother quite plainly, 'Leonardo, it is not you I wish to speak to but my daughter-in-law-to-be, your delightful Jodi. You have had her to yourself for quite long enough. Put her on the phone to me this minute, if you please, whilst I tell her about this wonderful shop for all things *bambino* in Milan.'

EPILOGUE

'AND you still intend to teach at your school?'

Over her mother-in-law's head Jodi smiled into Leo's eyes as Luisa Jefferson cooed ecstatically over the bundle that was her baby grandson.

It was Leo and Jodi's wedding anniversary and they had flown out to Italy to stay with Leo's parents.

'For the time being, but only on a part-time basis,' Jodi replied.

All the letters of support she had received from her pupils' parents had thrilled Jodi, and, as she and Leo had agreed, she owed it to everyone who had supported her to stay on at the school until the right kind of replacement for her had been found.

'After all,' she had smiled to Leo, 'our own children will be going there.'

Leo had bought Ashton House, and Jodi had spent all her free time in the months before baby Nicholas Lorenzo's birth organising its renovation and redecoration.

Leo's parents had flown over to Frampton from Italy for the baby's birth, and a special extra guest had been invited to the large family christening, much to Leo's wry amusement and his mother's open delight.

'Her name is Maria, and she says that she will make a special potion for you to drink that will guarantee the happiness of you and Leonardo and your children,' Luisa

Jefferson had whispered to Jodi when she had introduced her village's wise woman to her.

'My happiness is already guaranteed,' Jodi had responded with a shining smile of trust and love in her husband's direction. 'Just so long as I have Leo!'

The world's bestselling romance series.

Seduction and Passion Guaranteed!

**They're gorgeous, they're glamorous...
and they're getting married!**

Be our VIP guest at two of the most-talked-about
weddings of the decade—lavish ceremonies where the
cream of society gather to celebrate these marriages
in dazzling international settings.

Welcome to the sensuous, scandalous world
of the rich, royal and renowned!

SOCIETY WEDDINGS
Two original short stories in one volume:

Promised to the Sheikh
by *Sharon Kendrick*

The Duke's Secret Wife
by *Kate Walker*
on sale August, #2268

**Pick up a Harlequin Presents® novel and you will
enter a world of spine-tingling passion and
provocative, tantalizing romance!**

*Available wherever
Harlequin books
are sold.*

More fabulous reading from
the Queen of Sizzle!

LORI
FOSTER

with

Forever
and Always

Back by popular demand are the scintillating stories of
Gabe and Jordan Buckhorn. They're gorgeous, sexy
and single…at least for now!

Available wherever books are sold—September 2002.

And look for Lori's ***brand-new*** single title,
CASEY in early 2003

The world's bestselling romance series.

HARLEQUIN®
Presents~

Seduction and Passion Guaranteed!

A new trilogy by **Carole Mortimer**

BACHELOR COUSINS

Three cousins of Scottish descent...they're male, millionaires and marriageable!

Meet Logan, Fergus and Brice, three tall, dark, handsome men about town. They've made their millions in London, but their hearts belong to the heather-clad hills of their grandfather McDonald's Scottish estate.

Logan, Fergus and Brice are about to give up their keenly fought-for bachelor status for three wonderful women— laugh, cry and read all about their trials and tribulations in their pursuit of love.

To Marry McKenzie
On-sale July, #2261

Look out for:
To Marry McCloud
On-sale August, #2267

To Marry McAllister
On-sale September, #2273

Pick up a Harlequin Presents novel and you will enter a world of spine-tingling passion and provocative, tantalizing romance!

HARLEQUIN®
Makes any time special®

*Available wherever
Harlequin books
are sold.*

Coming in July!
Top Harlequin® Presents author

Sandra Marton

Brings you a brand-new, spin-off
to her miniseries, *The Barons*

Raising the Stakes

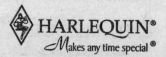

Attorney Gray Baron has come to Las Vegas on a mission to find
a woman—Dawn Lincoln Kittredge—the long-lost grandchild of
his uncle Jonas Baron. And when he finds her, an undeniable
passion ignites between them.

A powerful and dramatic read!

Look for it in stores, July 2002.

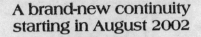

The world's bestselling romance series.

HARLEQUIN®
Presents

Seduction and Passion Guaranteed!

GREEK TYCOONS

They're the men who have everything—except a bride...

Wealth, power, charm—what else could a
heart-stoppingly handsome tycoon need? In the
GREEK TYCOONS miniseries you have already
been introduced to some gorgeous Greek
multimillionaires who are in need of wives.

Bestselling author *Jacqueline Baird* presents

THE GREEK TYCOON'S REVENGE
Harlequin Presents, #2266
Available in August

Marcus had found Eloise and he wants revenge—by
making Eloise his mistress for one year!

This tycoon has met his match, and he's decided he *has* to
have her...*whatever* that takes!

**Pick up a Harlequin Presents® novel and you will
enter a world of spine-tingling passion and
provocative, tantalizing romance!**

HARLEQUIN®
Makes any time special ®

*Available wherever
Harlequin books
are sold.*

Visit us at www.eHarlequin.com

HPGT07